Blind *Justice*

DEDICATION

First and foremost, thanks be to God for giving me the creativity and the confidence to share my work with the world. To my Mom and Brothers, words cannot articulate my appreciation. Without trepidation, you join me on my journeys; oftentimes, not knowing where you were going. To my other Mother, thank you for sharing your wisdom and spiritual guidance. To my friends, who are also my family, thank you for showering me with your love and support!

I would be remiss if I did not say thank you to Benton, who, after reading an excerpt of one chapter, encouraged me to share my imagination; and for designing my cover.

Blind *Justice*

*Where Love, Passion,
and the Law Await You...*

DD Roberts

ISBN: 978-0-578-84128-1

Contact us for bulk orders.
ddrobertsbooks.com
hello@ddrobertsbooks.com.

DISCLAIMER

This is a work of fiction. Names, characters, businesses, places, events, locales, and incidents are the products of the author's imagination or used fictitiously. Any resemblance to actual persons, living or dead, or actual events is purely coincidental.

Help support Human Trafficking—a portion of the proceeds will be contributed to Tabitha's House, a nonprofit organization working to assist all people affected by human trafficking.

Table of Contents

CHAPTER 1

Taylor and Isaiah Meet

"Welcome back, Ms. Alexander."

Taylor Alexander's energetic smile greets the Portman as she exits her flagship British luxury sports car, catching the skirt of her dress that the crisp night breeze blew open. She returned on a late flight from a weeklong trip to Los Angeles, where she serves as lead trial counsel on a legal case. "Good evening, Sir," she greets the poised doorman and enters the revolving doorway. Taylor's heels click as she sashays across the stylish lobby's marble floor to the elevator bay leading to her penthouse condo.

When the elevator opens right into her condo, the harmonious sounds of jazz from the built-in speakers and the potent perfume of Oriental Lilies welcome her. She envelops the feeling of home, noticing the bottle of red wine breathing on the counter and her favorite truffles next to it. Stepping out of her stilettos and laying her attaché on the countertop, she indulges in a truffle. Inhaling the aroma of blackberries and licorice, she pours a glass of her favorite Bordeaux. The fenestrated walls draw her to the stunning view of the city's skyline. "If Mr. Hunt weren't 75 years old and married, I'd marry him," Taylor says out loud, standing in front of the window.

Taylor's family employed Mr. Hunt all of her life. He made a deathbed promise to her father to look out for her after his death. Mr. Hunt is more than an employee; she has an abundance of respect for him. He knows everything about her and, in some ways, more than her father. From a young girl, Mr. Hunt looked after her and continues to do so in adulthood. When she returns from business trips, he prepares her favorites to ease the tension of travel. She loves him for his kindness. Not only did he nurture her through losing her father, but he also guided her as a young girl with life's simple ordeals—and still does.

A few weeks before Taylor's high-school graduation, her father—Robert Taylor Alexander, owner and CEO of Alexander Legal Services, a global leader in legal consulting—died when the company plane crashed returning from London. Taylor's grief was insurmountable; she did not sleep and barely ate for months. Mr. Hunt was her rock through all of it. She'd never met her mom, who died giving birth to her. Her grief caused her to skip high school graduation. And she took a gap year from college to cope with her loss—soul searching and backpacking in Asia. The tragic death of her father still causes an ache in the pit of her stomach. Will the pain ever go away? He was her go-to person and the best dad. As she gazes into the night, she relives fond memories of her dad, from learning to comb her hair to arguing over wearing lip-gloss to the length of her skirt. Oh, and her first date—he was hilarious! He dragged Coltrane with him to spy on her, hiding in the back of the movie theatre, blowing his cover when he sent Coltrane to tell her date to remove his arm from her neck. She laughs at the reminiscences. I miss you, Daddy.

Taylor inherited many traits from her dad, not just her namesake. He taught her how to write her name, ride a bike, and say her prayers. When it came time to train her for the debate team, the attorney in him was ecstatic. His coaching made her a fierce debater. She was destined to be a lawyer, having been groomed by Robert Taylor Alexander from a young age. When she was supposed to be finishing her homework, she would sneak to listen in on arbitrations from her father's office's adjoining room. When he allowed her to sit in the courtroom for one of his trials, she knew she would be a lawyer from that day. I am going to be just like him. She even recreated her desk in her bedroom to mimic his. One of her finest memoirs—and their last shared moment—was her first visit to a vineyard. Her dad was a sommelier, so she learned everything she knows about wine from him.

Taylor's phone rings, interrupting her trip down memory lane. "Hi, Mr. Hunt." He calls to ensure she made it in safely.

"Good evening, young lady. You all tucked away safely." Taylor's heart warms at the profound wisdom in his voice.

"Yes, sir, I did. And thank you for opening the wine." She still held the glass in her hand.

"Dinner is in the fridge if you're hungry." Mr. Hunt sounds like the grandpa Taylor never knew instead of her employee.

"Thank you, Mr. Hunt. I'll have it tomorrow. Extend my appreciation to Mrs. Hunt." Taylor never met Mrs. Hunt, but Mr. Hunt came alive when he spoke of her. And there is always a gift or token from him that resembles a woman's touch.

"I sure will. You get some rest, now." And Mr. Hunt ends the call. Taylor savors the kind moments because Mr. Hunt treats her like a granddaughter, not his employer. She appreciates all he does for her—from cooking her meals because she can't boil an egg, to giving her relationship advice, to helping her cope with her father's death. Taylor leans heavily on her faith in God—her dad made sure they worshiped every Sunday, from prayer service to Sunday school to worship service. But it was Mr. Hunt's guidance and protection and her best friends Dulaney and Coltrane that helped her survive the loss of her father.

Taylor met Dulaney and Coltrane in third grade, and they were inseparable ever since. It seems like yesterday, as she recalls, the morning they became friends. Taylor's dad was on a conference call earlier that morning, making her one of the last to arrive at school. Please don't let all the good seats be taken. She wanted the best front-row seat. She panted as she hurried down the hallway to her third-grade class. When Taylor walked through the class-room door, she was rattled. Dulaney was sitting at her front-row desk, her ponytails dangling. Students filed into the classroom, bumping into her. She stood frozen in the doorway. Then came the challenge. "You are in my seat!" With one hand on her hip, she stared at Dulaney, pleading for kindheartedness. The young girls banter over the seat quieted the classroom—all eyes on them. Dulaney did not want her teacher's discipline on the first day of school. Her mother wouldn't appreciate it. So she let Taylor have the desk, but not without letting Taylor know the desk wasn't hers to claim.

This was Coltrane's moment to demonstrate chivalry. He graciously offered Dulaney his desk and moved to the end of the row, but not before scribbling a note, leaving it on the desk for Dulaney to read.

Will you sit with me at lunch?

☐Yes ☐No ☐Maybe

As a peace offering, Taylor gave him a superhero pencil. That was the beginning of the trio.

Dulaney and Coltrane began their careers while Taylor went to law school. Coltrane's dream of becoming a sports agent recruiting the best talent came true, while Dulaney begrudgingly clerked for a US District Court Judge. At the same time, she strategized on getting signed by a reputable record label. Music is in her DNA; it's the only thing she loves more than life itself (except Coltrane). She ultimately lands a record deal and becomes one of the finest neo/soul artists in the industry.

When Taylor returned refreshed and rejuvenated from Asia, her sole focus was graduating college and getting her Juris Doctorate. Years later, the faculty honors her hard work, and she graduates Magna Cum Laude. Taylor postponed taking over as CEO of her father's firm, ALS, to pursue her passion for working in the juvenile justice system. Using her resources, she focused on her vision of building a place for inner-city youth to concentrate on math, science, and the arts. Her life's goal is to affect change in the lives of many boys and girls, but she'd be elated if she reaches one.

Taylor sat for the bar exam in Georgia and Washington, DC, and is licensed to practice law in both states. Although she hasn't accepted her position as CEO of the family's firm, Taylor consults on high-profile cases for the firm. She tries cases pro hac vice—meaning, a lawyer not admitted to practice in a specific jurisdiction may do so in a particular case in the unlicensed jurisdiction. She is one of the best trial lawyers and recently partnered with an Atlanta-based firm to try a case originating out of its Los Angeles office.

Litigating the case in Los Angeles presents Taylor with a significant challenge. How will she keep her non-profit organization operating effectively in Georgia while she spends eight weeks in Los Angeles? It's one thing to video-conference with Dulaney, but her Center needs a physical presence to support the kids' needs. She has to figure this out, and soon. In the meantime, she has an invitation to a fundraiser where only the elite in the political arena will be in attendance. And tonight, she rolls solo.

Taylor had yet to decide between the simple but elegant strapless nude dress and the allusive, custom tuxedo-style navy dress. Her glam squad arrives soon for hair and makeup. But first, she relaxes in a champagne bubble bath listening to contemporary jazz.

Taylor steps out of the limo, momentarily inhaling the night air before entering the building. As she enters the room filled with egos, Taylor glances at her reflection in the mirrored wall. The custom tuxedo-style navy dress was the right choice, complemented by the stilettos, extenuating her attractive legs. The glam squad was flawless with hair & makeup—a sleek ponytail met the small of her back and dramatic eyes with a nude lip. Taylor slides a glass of champagne off a server's tray and escapes through a small sliding door leading to a small balcony. One should probably not stand on the ledge, but the night air is brisk and helps unravel a million thoughts entangled in her mind. She sips her champagne, and the sensation of the fresh air calms her entrapped thoughts. Out of nowhere, this deep, rousing voice meddles with the madness in her mind. "Are you considering jumping? You're too pretty to splatter over the concrete."

Startled at the question and the voice, Taylor toys with her intruder. "And why would I jump?" Without giving him a chance to respond to the rhetorical question, Taylor mocks, "Just escaping the egos in the room."

"You appear to be a sharpshooter—no offense—are you telling me you don't have an ego of your own?" the compelling voice contests Taylor.

Sizing the man with a near-erotic voice, Taylor probes, "Sharpshooter, care to elaborate?"

He leans into the balcony, remaining as cool as the other side of the pillow, and flatters her. "You are beautiful and look amazing! You're at an invitation-only, black-tie affair— appear to be alone—yet not intimidated. Your demeanor exudes confidence. Not only didn't you back down at my wisecrack, but you also appear to have fun embracing it. You are quick on your feet. I'd say you're a sharpshooter." His words flow like a melody to a seductive beat without pause or interruption as he flirts with Taylor.

She couldn't discern if it's the warmth of his body close to hers or the eloquently spoken words causing the goose-bumps to rise on her arm. Oh dear God, do not let this man come closer. It is clear the gentleman is flirting. "Do you always turn up the charm when you've put your foot in your mouth?" Strong chemistry flows between them.

"Don't confuse confidence for charm." He fringes on arrogance, but his sensual smile balances his cockiness. "Do you think I am charming?" She is downright gorgeous.

"I reserve the right to not answer on the grounds it may incriminate me." The lawyer in Taylor surfaces as her dark, sultry eyes hold his gaze.

"Ah, hah. You're a lawyer?" His eyes dash away before she notices the lust in them. He wants to run his hands up her stunning legs, inside the slit of her dress, past her curvy waist until they cup the perfectly sized breast hidden under the elegant dress she wears.

Taylor's thoughts travel as she appreciates the statue standing before her. He is striking, has a mind-blowing physique, and the black tux covering every muscle appears tailor-made. Lord, what do his muscles look like outside of his jacket. His brown eyes sparkle and that damn smile. Geez! "I neither confirm nor deny that allegation." Taylor can't contain her humor.

"Okay, Counselor." He laughs lightly and throws up his hands in defeat. "My name is Isaiah Myers," he extends his hand to shake hers.

Meeting his motion, she extends her hand, "Taylor Alexander." I need to escape this delightful statue before I lose all my senses. His mannerisms intrigue Taylor, and although he borders on egotism, he is confident and easy on the eyes.

"It's a pleasure to meet you, Ms. Alexander. Would you like another drink?" Isaiah asks politely.

"No, thank you. I should get back in and shake a few hands. It's nice meeting you." Taylor holds her breath, sliding by his tall, dark, and handsome frame, and re-enters the ballroom. She makes her way toward the mayor until the district attorney intercepts her. As he does with every conversation, the DA coaxes Taylor to join his office.

"When will you join my team, young lady? Your father would be proud of you." He gently hugs Taylor and tells her he's proud of the work she's doing with the community's youth.

As he releases her from the hug, "Thank you, sir, but my youth need me to keep them out of your folks' hands." Taylor jokes but means every word.

The District Attorney laughs, asking, "Making your way to the Mayor?"

"Sure am," Taylor responds.

"I'm heading that way myself. I'll walk with you." The DA extends his arm as if to a debutante and escorts her across the ballroom. Taylor spends the rest of the night in discussions with the DA and Mayor. "You know, Ms. Alexander, my nephew is in town. I'd like to introduce him to you." Before Taylor objects, the mayor summons his nephew. Much to Taylor's surprise, his nephew is Isaiah—the fine-looking, confident gentleman from the balcony.

The mayor smiles with esteem as Isaiah approaches. "Isaiah, I'd like you to meet the finest trial lawyer on the east and west coasts." There is a slight awkwardness as Isaiah fixates on Taylor.

His conversation with Taylor is etched in his mind since meeting her on the balcony. He reminds her, "I see you're still shaking hands." These political fundraisers are usually the epitome of boredom. But tonight, he meets a woman who piqued his interest, and she stands before him with his Uncle. This is a night to remember.

Looking between Isaiah and Taylor bewildered, Mayor Sellect asks, "Have you two met?"

Isaiah smiles devilishly, "Yes, she was jumping over the ledge of the balcony, and I rescued her." The mayor's eyes widen, and he turns red. Befuddled by Isaiah's comment, he looks at Taylor utterly confused. Isaiah winks at his Uncle to relax his concern before turning his attention to Taylor, "So, you are a lawyer?"

Blurting out without giving Taylor a chance, "Yes, she is, and one of the best," the mayor speaks.

"It's nice to meet you again, Mr. Myers," Taylor offers.

Reluctantly, Isaiah embraces Taylor in a hug. A shock of static flickers between them, and she quickly backs away. Like her, Isaiah feels the shock wave and releases the hold. "I'm sorry, but I don't shake the hands of beautiful ladies twice," Isaiah says uncomfortably. The moderator taps the microphone, gaining the crowd's attention. "Good evening, ladies and gentlemen. I hope everyone is having a great time. Before we hear the melodic sounds of Mr. Will Downing, I ask that you wrap up your pledge goals. So get your pens out. Write your pledges on the back of your place cards. Please give generously so we can charitably support new programs focused on the development of our youth. Thank you so much and enjoy your evening."

The ballroom is loud as everyone makes their way to their tables to complete their pledges. When Taylor finalizes her pledge amount, she announces, "I'll say good evening to you, gentlemen." She addresses the mayor, "Mr. Mayor; I will be in touch." The mayor tips his glass to her, and she walks away. Isaiah watches her, immobile for a minute—the sway of her hips and those stunning legs in high heels. She ignites his senses. Before he knew it, his legs moved to catch up to her.

Isaiah gently touches Taylor's elbow to gain her attention. "May I walk you to your car?"

The bizarre moment when electricity flickered between them has Taylor self-conscious. What if he hugs her again? Does she want to feel those shock waves with him? She rejects Isaiah's request. "Thank you, but my driver is waiting. Enjoy the rest of your evening." Taylor turns on the heel of her shoe like a ballerina and strides, calling attention to her legs. With every step, the elegance of the way her body moves and the ponytail swinging in rhythm hypnotizes Isaiah. Taylor feels him watching her. As she turns to the elevator, she waves a few fingers as if stroking a chord on the piano to say bye.

On Sunday morning, the whistling sound of the teakettle awakens Taylor. She believes she is dreaming, but a silhouette resembling her best friend in a hunter-green dress with pearls bounces off the windows. She grudgingly sits up in bed and thinks, "I'm late for church." Then her attention goes back to the shadow, realizing it is Dulaney in her kitchen. I will remove her access. She drags herself out of bed into the kitchen and sits at the wet bar. "Good morning. Why are you brewing tea in my kitchen?" Taylor mumbles to Dulaney.

Not turning around to face Taylor, Dulaney retrieves the sweetener and two teacups as she greets her best friend. "One, because I owe you an apology, and two, because my best friend leaves for Los Angeles tomorrow. And, I thought you'd be ready for church. Late-night?"

Sitting on the stool at her breakfast bar with her head synced into her palms, Taylor mutters, "Not really. I am concerned about leaving the Foundation unattended, and because of that, I haven't focused on the case." Shifting to

11

her sarcastic tone, Taylor spouts at Dulaney, "Thank you for reminding me I leave tomorrow, which also reminds me I haven't packed a pair of panties." Taylor sips the tea Dulaney placed before her. "But, I met a fine brother at the Mayor's ball last night."

From the opposite side of the bar, Dulaney spills her tea, hearing Taylor's last statement. "You are supposed to lead with that. Who?" It's Dulaney's turn to interrogate.

"He's the Mayor's nephew, lives in Los Angeles..." Dulaney cuts her off mid-sentence.

"Well, isn't that opportune?"

"This is good, thank you," Taylor savors the tea before sharing. "He is exquisite. He has the most beautiful dark eyes a man could possess and perfect angles defining his handsome face. And then there are his muscles—sensuous, chiseled lines that make an impressive and sinfully pleasing body. Oh, and his smile—it's a smirk, and a smile combined—but it's dazzling. The hairs on my arms rose."

"Damn!" Dulaney is animated. She does not recall any man who exhilarated Taylor. She hasn't dated much, not seriously. Between ALS and the Foundation, Taylor is either in a meeting or preparing for a trial. She rarely allows social time. The few times she did date, Dulaney never heard her describe anyone the way she just did. "Are you going to see him again?"

"It was a professional event. We didn't exchange numbers." Dulaney could hear a tinge of regret in Taylor's voice. Why didn't I let him walk me to the car? Maybe he would've asked for my number.

"Why not?" Dulaney couldn't make sense of what her friend said. First, she describes a good-looking man who

12

awakens something in her but then says she didn't give him her number. "Is he a murderer?"

She and Taylor exchange ensnared faces before Taylor pouts. "Don't be silly!" Taylor fumbles with the teacup before admitting, "His stare scorched my skin. It was like an electrical current caressed our bodies when we hugged. I don't know; I guess I dismissed it as sexual suppression. So when he asked to walk me to my car, I told him, no, thank you."

"You are unbelievable!" Dulaney is jolted by what she heard. "What if you run into him in LA?"

"I doubt I'll run into him in LA." Taylor thought the perfect way to change this conversation. "Speaking of LA, I have things to do to prepare for tomorrow's departure." Taylor's demeanor shifts from the perky, giggly girl talking about a guy to distress. And Dulaney recognizes it.

"Take a few pieces to get you through your first week. I will rummage through your closet and send clothes to you later." Dulaney braces herself for Taylor's reaction to her next statement. "As for the Foundation—I'm just throwing it out there—did you consider asking Coltrane to oversee things while you're gone?" Dulaney shrugs her neck into her shoulders.

Stumped, Taylor exclaims, "Who are you? And what did you do with my best friend?" Taylor played mediator between Dulaney and Coltrane for as long as she remembers, dating back to grade school. It was exhausting. Two years ago, she gave them both a two-week notice and resigned her unofficial position as mediator. Dulaney and Coltrane haven't spoken since. Dulaney was his everything—he cherished her since third grade. It wasn't until college, freshman year, she succumbed to his fervent advances. He became her proxy BFF since Taylor was in Asia coping with the loss of her dad. But it all went to hell in a handbasket in one night.

Three years ago, Coltrane and Dulaney had plans to see a Broadway show in NYC on her birthday. It was the height of football season—the playoffs—and Coltrane's sports management empire's busiest season. The week of Dulaney's birthday, he flew from city to city meeting after meeting preparing for the Super Bowl. The only way he wasn't in the stadium on Super Bowl Sunday was if it collapsed.

All hell broke loose, and Coltrane's life forever changed, leaving Dulaney alone and heartbroken. On the day he was to celebrate Dulaney's birthday, Coltrane received a life-altering call he could never have imagined. He borrowed his client's private jet and arranged for Dulaney's pickup in Atlanta. Instead of celebrating life with the girl of his dreams, that phone call redirected him to Charlotte. He was dumbfounded at the news he received. His mental psyche went into shock—as if he stepped out of his body into someone else's life. Given the sudden shift in his mental capacity, calling Dulaney never crossed his mind. He did a few days later, and it's been a downward spiral since.

Dulaney was inconsolable. In one night, her world shattered. The man who was to be her forever was now, not ever. Dulaney ultimately forgave Coltrane but had not seen or spoken to him in two years. She believed it was best, particularly for him; he had a brand new world to figure out.

"I know... I know. It's weird coming from me. But you need to focus on your case, not worry about the Foundation. He's capable and he won't mind." Dulaney convinces Taylor.

Taylor knows Coltrane can and will oversee her Foundation. She didn't want to hurt Dulaney's feelings by asking him. "But will you mind?" Taylor asks in her most sincere voice. She maintains her friendships with them since she resigned as their unofficial mediator. They were once a trifecta; now, it is different. But Taylor remains loyal to both her friends.

"I'm a big girl. Do what's best for your case, the Foundation, and your sanity. Just don't ask me to help him." Dulaney implores. She loved Coltrane since the day he stopped her pencil from rolling under the desk. He was kind and the perfect gentleman, even at such a young age. He gave her his seat in class when Taylor insisted Dulaney took hers, which wasn't the case.

"Deal. I'll call him now." Taylor excitedly jumped off the barstool.

"Will you wait until I am gone? Are you coming to church?" Dulaney squeals.

"Of course! God just solved two of my three problems. We'll be a few minutes late, but I'll be ready in 20 minutes." Taylor pretends to play hopscotch on an imaginary boundary on her floor as she skips to the shower, humming a musical sound only she recognizes.

Dulaney and Taylor discreetly try to slide into the back section of the sanctuary, but the male usher guides them to the middle. Praise and worship is in high gear as the choir leads the congregation to upbeat sounds of praise. Dulaney is already moving to the beat, as this is one of her favorites. When she places her bag under the chair, her eyes land on Coltrane at the end of the row. Why is he here? This isn't his church. Dulaney grabs her handbag and hurries out of the cathedral, disheveled. She hadn't seen Coltrane in years, but his presence fueled her. She pants heavily as the sight of him stirs pent-up passion.

Taylor was so engrossed in the praise she didn't notice Dulaney leave. She sits when the choir sings How Great is our God, but Dulaney's seat is empty with no sign of her. The vibration of her cell phone alerts her to Dulaney's message. She left. It's during visitor's acknowledgment when Taylor grasps why Dulaney left service.

It dawns on Taylor as service draws to a close; she is stranded. She rode to church with Dulaney. Immediately after the benediction, Coltrane strides in her direction. With no greeting, "Is everything okay with Dulaney?" Coltrane queries Taylor.

"Good morning to you, too!" Thinking fast and not fidgeting, "She has an unsettled stomach," Taylor lies. She couldn't believe she just lied in church. She will kill Dulaney.

"Oh, okay," is all Coltrane says. He looks questionably at Taylor to see if she fiddles. They all know each other's telltale signs, and that's Taylor's when she isn't telling the truth.

Determined not to reveal she just deceived, Taylor shifts the conversation. "Can a girl in a lower tax bracket get a ride home?" Taylor pokes Coltrane on the shoulder. "I rode with Dulaney."

Coltrane creates an opportunity to talk about Dulaney. "Sure. Do you have time for brunch? It's been a minute since we kicked it." He is determined to find out what's going on with Dulaney. There's no better person to interrogate but the Counselor, who is her best friend.

After Coltrane opens the passenger door for Taylor, he slides behind the wheel. Looking in Taylor's direction, he asks, "Flying Biscuit, Buttermilk Kitchen, or J Christopher's?"

"Buttermilk Kitchen," Taylor doesn't hesitate. It is one of her favorite brunch spots. It is a little blue house that's always packed and always has a line, but it is well worth the wait. Its menu is filled with southern cuisine, and they make everything from scratch with all local ingredients. As Coltrane proceeds out of the parking lot and onto the interstate en route to Buttermilk Kitchen, Taylor pleads. "So, Mr. Billionaire, how much time do you have on your schedule the next eight weeks?"

"What's going on?" Coltrane asks inquisitively.

Taylor continues her petition. "I have a trial in Los Angeles and it's on the docket for eight weeks. My departure is scheduled for tomorrow but the Foundation will be left unattended. I know of no better person to oversee it in my absence than Vous."

Coltrane's wondering what's up with Dulaney. "Isn't D on your Board? Why can't she step in?"

"She can't; she's got stuff going on." Taylor is determined not to open doors or reveal information, answering only the question asked.

"What stuff? What's going on with her, Tay?" Coltrane presses. He loved Dulaney since grade school, and he loves her still. But Dulaney will not talk to him, see him, or respond to him in any way. He's sent flowers, bought jewelry, a baby grand piano, and every other imaginable thing for the past two years to show her he's sorry. Dulaney's stubbornness prevailed. Not only did she reject every gesture, but she also refused to hear him out.

"Trane, don't put me in the middle. That's y'all stuff. But I need your help. Don't you think I'd have her if she could?" Taylor becomes annoyed at Coltrane's probing.

Breaking the ice before the tension grows further, "I thought you knew of no better person?" Coltrane laughs.

"You are the better person. She's the best person; she just can't step in right now." Taylor explains. "Can you?"

Negotiation is his specialty, and this is a time when he'd leverage that skill. But carefully, the Counselor isn't one to cross. "Provide my secretary with your daily calendar. You can brief me at brunch. But, on one condition." Coltrane bargains.

"What's that?" Taylor asks, puzzled.

"Tell me what's going on with Dulaney." Coltrane spurts before he changes his mind. He knows he risks pissing off Taylor. It is worth it to him.

"I won't overstep the boundaries you ask me to cross." The disappointment in Taylor's voice is apparent.

Neither spoke for the rest of the ride. When they approach their exit, Taylor breaks the silence, suggesting they grab something from the coffee shop on the corner. Coltrane's only response is swerving the exclusive GT sports car into the parking lot and circling the drive-thru. He orders, pays the young lady at the window, and hands Taylor a Caramel Macchiato. She thanks him, and the ride to Taylor's home is silent, except for the music seeping through the speakers.

Coltrane pulls into the circular driveway of Taylor's building. "Thanks again for the coffee and the ride." Taylor exits the car; disappointment is evident.

"You're welcome."

As Taylor makes her way to the elevator, the same thoughts navigating the intricacies of her mind the night before resurfaces with a vengeance. Gracious Father, there has to be a way to do it all. Surely I can try a case in Los Angeles and run a Foundation in Atlanta. After all, you spoke the world into existence in seven days. Her thoughts make her brain their speedway. She steps into the foyer of her home, slides down the side of the wall, dropping everything except her coffee to the floor, and prays.

Father, I stand on your word. Some trust in chariots and some in horses, but I trust and believe in the name of Jesus. I'm calling on you, Father; hear my cry. You said your word does not return to you void. You said whatever I ask in prayer, believing, I shall receive it. Well, Father, I ask boldly that my mountain be moved. God, this is your work. I am carrying out the assignment you gave me. You prepared me for this, and you said you'd build the character to match the assignment. So, Father, I thank you for removing all obstacles, tearing down every stronghold, and destroying every yoke. Touch the heart of the one who will keep the Foundation operating while I am in LA and cause that one to align with the work you're doing. I declare it so. In the matchless name of Jesus Christ, I pray. Amen, Amen, and Amen.

When she finishes her prayer, Taylor sits against the wall in silence and finishes her Caramel Macchiato. After, she packs for LA. She packs only enough for one week, holding Dulaney to her word to send her clothes. She clears the teacups and prepares a light lunch. Heading into her home office off of the foyer, she hears her phone buzzing in her purse. It's on the floor where she dropped it earlier. She retrieves her phone from the bottom of her handbag, noticing two missed calls from Dulaney. This is the third. Taylor will call her friend back after she takes a cursory review of the discovery. The text tone from her phone interrupts her. It's from Coltrane and reads, *Have your sect send your cal to mine. I need a briefing since you bailed on brunch. Touch base later. Pray for your traveling grace, and I'm sorry.*

Teary-eyed, Taylor looks to heaven and thanks to God for not forsaking her. She prepares the briefing for Coltrane. Several hours later, Taylor shuts down all electronics in her office, stuffs her attaché with case files, and breathes a sigh of relief. She is prepared for LA. It's naptime.

The door chimes wake Taylor. Mr. Hunt is off today, and she's uncertain of the instructions he gave the concierge? She pulls herself off the sofa and stumbles to the entry. The delivery shocks her. The concierge's voice comes from behind the arrangement, "Delivery for you, Ms. Alexander." Her confused look is apparent as she accepts the Asian-inspired arrangement that includes orange lilies, ti leaves, and bamboo stems. Who sent her flowers? She places them on the table in the foyer and reaches for the card. It was my pleasure to rescue you from the ledge. Taylor laughs hysterically. The concierge smiles as he exits. "Thank you."

She wonders how Isaiah knows where she lives? She never lists her home address on anything, only her ALS office address. I suppose if you're the mayor's nephew, surely you can get your hands on an address. She'll send him a thank you note later. Right now, it is time to deal with her best friend.

She changes into sweats and sneakers. As she exits her building, Coltrane's driver rounds the circular driveway. "Ms. Alexander, Mr. Coltrane asked me to stop by to get some files and keys from you. He said you know the details."

Baffled because Coltrane's text did not indicate he'd send for anything, Taylor explains. "Yes, I am aware of the details, but that information is at my youth center."

Seeming unbothered by the puzzled look on Taylor's face, "I don't mind going to your office, Ms. Alexander. Is someone there who knows what to give me?" Mr. Freeman asks.

Of course, no one is at her office—it's Sunday. While she sometimes works on Sunday afternoons, seldom does she ask her assistant to do so. "No, sir. If you don't mind, you can take me to the office. I can get them. It's downtown near the courthouse." Taylor responds, peering through the half-lowered window of the black SUV.

"Yes, ma'am. I can do that." And the driver gets out to open the door for Taylor. She waves to the Portman not to retrieve her car and climbs into the SUV.

Taylor is beyond grateful God answered her prayer and touched Coltrane's heart. They arrive at Garnett Street, and Taylor informs the driver she'd only be a short while. She hurries into her office, gathers essential files, and as she does so, thoughts flood her head. Why does he want the files away from the office if he will come by daily? She doesn't allow the assumption to paralyze her, but places the files in an empty briefcase and heads back to the SUV.

Standing on the outside of the vehicle, obviously waiting for Taylor to return, Mr. Freeman inquires. "May I return you to your home, Ms. Alexander?"

Knowing she was headed to Dulaney when Mr. Freeman surprisingly arrived at her building, "No, sir. Do you mind taking me to 17th Street?"

"No, ma'am; not at all." Mr. Freeman opens the door, allowing Taylor into the vehicle. After securing his seat belt, he maneuvers toward midtown en route to 17th Street. When they reach the building, Taylor thanks him, hands over an envelope where she'd secured the keys to her office, and gestures to the briefcase on the back seat. She exits the vehicle and enters the building en route to the 22nd floor, where her friend resides. She greets the concierge who knows Taylor, so she doesn't bother her with protocol, and Taylor continues to the elevator. When she reaches Dulaney's unit, she taps on the door. She rarely uses the fob to enter out of courtesy. Dulaney isn't expecting anyone, and no one called from downstairs, so she makes her way to the door and looks through the eyehole. When she notices Taylor, she springs the door open with, "I've been calling you all day. Where have you been?"

Taylor pushes past Dulaney and into the unit. "Oh no, you do not get to interrogate me. You abandoned me at church. To top it off, I lied in the church to cover you. You may not recognize your issues, my dear, but let me enlighten you. I suggest you tap into your inner self, self-reflect, and embrace your truths. You cannot keep hiding and running. For God's sake, what will it take for you to be honest with him; more importantly, be honest with yourself?" Taylor is gasping by the time she finishes.

Dulaney utters not a word, walks away from the door, and slouches back in the chaise lounge where she reads DD Robert's Blind Justice. Taylor is right in that she needs to face her challenges. She hasn't touched her music since the doctor's diagnosis more than a year ago. Music soothes her soul; yet, she avoids it because it also reminds her of Coltrane's many memories. He doesn't know of her diagnosis.

Taylor closes the door and follows Dulaney into the living room. She softly expresses, "D, you cannot keep doing this to yourself. It's not healthy. And it's not good for your health." She sits on the corner of the chaise to look at Dulaney, who is shutting down. "I haven't said anything, but it's getting progressively worse. I leave tomorrow and need to know you're taking care of yourself."

Mustering the strength to not shed the water fighting with her tear ducts, "I'll be fine. I'll send your clothes as I promised. Have a safe trip." Dulaney speaks determinedly, refusing to cry.

Recognizing Dulaney's attempt to contain her emotions—after all, this is her best friend. "D, don't do this." Using all the fibers of her being to maintain composure, "I'll be fine. Good luck with the trial, and safe travels." Dulaney fought back the tears.

Taylor knows Dulaney has shut down. This conversation is over. She hugs her best friend—who does not budge—tells her she loves her and leaves Dulaney to process her emotions. She'll call her after she lands in LA.

No sooner than the door closes behind Taylor does the floodgates open. Dulaney cries uncontrollably. A myriad of emotions flows through her. She does not know what to do with them. So she weeps, hoping God hears her silent prayer.

Chapter 2

Taylor Arrives in LA

Taylor lands in Los Angeles with an unsettled spirit. She checks her phone as the aircraft taxies to the gate. Dulaney hasn't responded to her texts. Taylor knows Dulaney's stubbornness all too well, but she needs to know her best friend is okay. It's been three years since the demise of Dulaney and Coltrane's relationship, yet Dulaney continues to run from him. It's time to stop and face her hurt. Dulaney needed to hear that, but is her timing off? Taylor and Dulaney argued a million times over but were never 2000 miles apart amidst a disagreement.

Taylor gets her carry-on from the overhead bin, exits the plane, and heads into the 88-degree weather. A gentleman stands next to a black SUV holding a sign with her name on it. When she gets close, he inquires, "Ms. Alexander?" She acknowledges him, and he retrieves her luggage, opening the back passenger door for her. In no time, they are on the 405 en route to the hotel.

The Westin Bonaventure Hotel & Suites is in the Financial District—a short walk from S. Flowers Street, the office location. If she caught a game, it's also within walking distance to the Staples Center. Taylor checks into her Huntington suite and prepares for an in-room massage, which she pre-arranged. The suite transforms into an oasis with scented candles, calming music, and fresh aromas. A selection of aromatherapy oils and room sprays line the small counter. After her massage, Taylor relaxes her body and quiets her mind in a detoxifying bath inspired by ancient rituals. This is precisely what she needs after the long flight and the stress of her unsettled conversation with Dulaney.

Famished after her pampering, Taylor devours a savory Asian chicken salad with sesame ginger dressing in the hotel restaurant. She finishes her lunch and enjoys a peaceful nap before heading to the office to focus on the task at hand—the upcoming trial. Her client is accused of attempted murder of a decorated police officer, but the pieces of the puzzle don't connect.

As Taylor approaches the twin tower skyscraper complex, she stops and admires the architectural décor. When she enters the lobby area, it is just as exquisite as its exterior. Taylor crosses the lobby to the elevator that takes her to the 25th-floor office. The receptionist welcomes Taylor and escorts her to a corner office. She smiles and offers, "This is where you'll live during your tenure with us." Windows with amazing views of downtown LA, a built-in bar, and exquisite furnishing make up the C-suite office. The fenestrated walls draw her to the stunning view of the city.

Establishing a relationship with the receptionist and showing a lighter side of her personality, Taylor jokes with her. "You mean I should give up my suite at The Westin?" They laugh.

"I'll let Mr. Daniels know you are here. And, I'll familiarize you with the libations—you know, the important stuff. But settle in, first. Would you like a bottle of water?" Taylor graciously accepts the water. The massage left her dehydrated. The receptionist returns with a bottle of water and Mr. Daniels.

Gesturing to showcase the corner office, Mr. Daniels greets Taylor. "I see Cathy has given you a tour. How was your flight?"

Taylor smiles at Cathy and shakes Mr. Daniels' hand. "Yes, she has. Thank you, Cathy. "The flight was long, but it's good to be on the west coast. How are you?"

"I couldn't be better," Mr. Daniels answers.

"Good. Are you ready to dive in?" Taylor asks.

Mr. Daniels proposes, "Why don't you use the afternoon to settle in, and we dive in tomorrow morning. Are you agreeable, Counselor?"

"Sounds like a plan," Taylor agrees. "I'll complete my review of the discovery this afternoon. Do you have space for me to create a war room?"

"I'll show you to the conference room where we review files and hold discussions." Mr. Daniels leads the way to the conference room.

The two lawyers engage in small talk before Mr. Daniels leaves Taylor to her review. She buries herself in the discovery the rest of the day. Where is the police report? What about the investigator's report? Why is necessary information missing from the file? The office is empty when she comes up for air; it's almost 7:30 p.m. She will review the pre-trial schedule at the hotel while she eats dinner. She'll call Dulaney again before she goes to bed.

Taylor woke up the next morning with the same thoughts she went to bed with—what's missing and why is the discovery incomplete. She lay in bed wishing she had time for an outdoor workout at Mt. Hollywood Peak. It beats the treadmill, but that's all time allows for this morning. She arrives at the office about 7:30 a.m. and gets cozy in the conference room, where she left the table covered in files, papers, and unanswered questions. She continues her review where she left off the evening before.

Mr. Daniels entered the conference room without Taylor noticing. Her focus is on piecing together the investigator's report, which is neither complete nor thorough. "Except that there's no plush showers or beds in this building, I'd ask if you slept here."

"Good morning." Taylor interrogates Mr. Daniels. "Let me ask, why is the investigator's report incomplete? And where is the arrest report? Has anyone interviewed the defendant? I didn't see a transcript of the interview in the discovery file."

"I will introduce you to our associate, John Hansen, who handled most of the discovery. He will answer your questions." Taylor frowns, wondering why Mr. Daniels offered his associate to answer her.

"Who is paying the defendant's legal fees?" she continues.

It is clear to Mr. Daniels Taylor isn't letting up. "Ms. Alexander, maybe you and I should have a cup of coffee and chat."

Mr. Daniels' suggestion troubles Taylor. "Making sense of the incomplete discovery is a priority. I don't see Mr. Boyd's Myers deposition transcript. Did the prosecutor take his deposition? And, I am concerned we don't have all the information we need to try this case. Do you honestly want me to stop to have coffee, Mr. Daniels?"

"Yes, that's correct," Mr. Daniels reiterates.

"Tell me, who's financing Mr. Myer's legal defense?"

Mr. Daniels is as stern as the first time he suggested coffee. "I'll share those details over coffee, Ms. Alexander."

Taylor isn't interested in coffee. Is the teacup in front of her invisible to him? But she is interested in why Mr. Daniels wants to chat privately. She rolls the high-back executive chair from the table, stands, and motions for Mr. Daniels to blaze the trail. Their trip to the coffee bar is silent. After ordering, Mr. Daniels points to a corner table away from the crowd. When seated, Taylor asks, "What are you not telling me?"

Mr. Daniels is as expressionless as he was in the conference room. He observes Taylor's non-verbal cues and recites her questions, responding to each. "You asked why the investigator's report is incomplete? The investigator's death occurred before he finished the report. Where is the arrest report? It's in the file. Has anyone interviewed the defendant, you asked? Myers was not deposed. Mayor Sellect retained our firm to represent Myers and recommended you lead our trial team. I believe that answers all your questions."

"Mayor Sellect? What?" Taylor is dumbfounded. "What is the Mayor of Atlanta's interest in this defendant?" She spoke to the Mayor twice in the past weeks; he never mentioned this case. Taylor suddenly feels there's more to this than what Mr. Daniels shares.

"It's his nephew, and..."

"His nephew! The Mayor's nephew allegedly shot a retired LAPD officer and left him to die in the Santa Monica Mountains?"

"You got it, Counselor." Mr. Daniels replies.

Mr. Daniels' affirmation disturbed Taylor, but he isn't fazed. "How did you convince the judge to grant bail?"

"I didn't. And that's all I am at liberty to say." You've got to be kidding me, she thought.

It annoys Taylor to learn the Mayor advocated for her to try this case but failed to mention it to her. This is a first. To add salt to the wound, the defendant is his nephew. "A police officer is shot and left for dead. The investigator is killed. And you're not at liberty to say? Should I be concerned? Am I next since I am litigating the case? Who is at liberty to say something? That's the person I want to talk to." Mr. Daniels gapes at Taylor but does not answer.

She stands—frustrated by the conversation—and asks, "Am I the lead trial lawyer because of my association with the Mayor?"

"Six degrees of separation," Mr. Daniels' attempt to lighten her mood fails. And the look on her face gives him cause for concern.

"I need to interview the defendant. Have Cathy notify him to come to the office at 4 o'clock today, please." Taylor left Mr. Daniels to his tea and stormed out of the building.

When Taylor returns to the office, Cathy informs her Hansen is in the conference room waiting. She walks into the room but doesn't introduce herself. "Fill me in. Let's start with the arrest report. Is the one in the discovery file the accurate arrest report? Could it be falsified?"

Hansen considers introducing himself. It isn't clear to him why she is stoic, so he opts to answer questions. "As best I know, it's the original arrest report."

Taylor is incensed by her conversation with Mr. Daniels. "Confirm it. And if it's not, get your hands on the arrest

30

report today, please." Hansen wonders what caused her overt hostility.

"Did the investigator share vital information before his death? Are you attuned to the investigation of his death? Get me whatever you can on that investigation." Taylor continues her grilling.

"Today?" Hansen japes to dismiss the tension. He felt like a 5th grader scolded by his teacher.

"Yes; today, if you don't mind. Is that a problem?" She doesn't bother to look up from the pile of papers.

"No problem. I'm on it." Hansen is off to carry out his orders.

Taylor remembers her request to interview the defendant as Hansen approaches the doorway. "Oh, I'm interviewing Mr. Myers at 4:00 p.m. today. Please don't be late." She barks as Hansen exits the conference room. He doesn't respond. As he passes Cathy's desk, he sneers, "She's a bulldog. I'll be back in a couple of hours. Got some investigating to do." Cathy waves and continues answering the phone.

Taylor mulls over the material in the discovery file. She cannot come to terms with why the Mayor did not mention the trial. He has never referred her to a case without briefing her. What is Mayor Sellect withholding from her? She has her work cut out, and it bothers her that neither the Mayor nor Mr. Daniels leveled with her. A thought interrupts Taylor's contemplation. She should interview Mr. Myers at the scene. It is unconventional, but it may prove worthwhile. She scurries to Cathy's desk. "Cathy, contact Mr. Myers and have him meet me at the scene. I'll interview him there."

Cathy looks at her apprehensively. "At the crime scene?"

"Yes." Taylor went back to the conference room to gather evidence. Files tucked within the elbow of her left arm, she grabs her handbag and heads out of the office, making her request to Cathy in stride. "Cathy, please call the car service for me. I'll be waiting at the curb."

"To go where?" Taylor is no longer in sight by the time Cathy looks up for her answer.

The Mulholland Drive gate is open when the driver arrives. The sweeping gravel road curves to the north side of the mountain, arriving at a junction beneath the summit. Continuing ahead, unpaved Mulholland Drive continues across the Santa Monica Mountains. The view is titillating.

During the drive, Taylor researched the mountains on Wikipedia and learned San Vicente Mountain was used to defend Los Angeles from Soviet missile attacks in the 1950s. The missiles were obsoleted, but the Santa Monica Mountains Conservancy preserved the site to share the history with visitors.

Taylor takes in the view, expanding in the opposite direction down the Encino Reservoir. She cannot fathom a crime scene. While waiting on Mr. Myers' arrival, Taylor takes a walk on the trail, enjoying the fresh air and exhilarating view. She made a quick run to the hotel for her sneakers while waiting on the car service to arrive.

Reenacting the details of the police report, she realizes something is missing. As Taylor imagines the scene depicted in the police report, she hears voices along the trail which isn't surprising. It is a two-mile hike following the unpaved portion of Mulholland Drive. It is peaceful—at least to her. Hansen and Mr. Daniels are out of breath approaching her, and she cannot contain her laughter. "Gentlemen, glad you can join me. Isn't the view heart-stopping?"

Hansen huffs and puffs for air. He isn't sure how to engage with Taylor as his first encounter bordered on contention. Mr. Daniels gazes over the peak as he pants. "It is, but my heart will stop if I must hike two-mile trails. Is Myers here?"

"No, but he has a few minutes before the top of the hour."

At that moment, Taylor hears two male voices nearing. One voice sounds familiar, but she knows no one in Los Angeles. Mr. Daniels points toward the two men. "Here's our client, now." Taylor's knees weaken. She is sure she tumbled over the cliff. Alongside the man whom Mr. Daniels points out as their client is the fine-looking, confident gentleman from the Mayor's ball. What the hell! A salacious grin covers his face. His gaze travels the length of her body, lingering on her lips. Her grip tightens damn near to pain as she clinches the pen in her hand.

Mr. Daniels places one hand on their client's shoulder, using the other to gesture to Taylor. "Myers, this is the trial attorney from Atlanta who leads your case, Ms. Taylor Alexander," Mr. Daniels announces like a proud father.

Boyd Myers extends his hand to shake Taylor's, but she is shocked into stillness. "Hello, Ms. Alexander. It's a pleasure to meet you. My uncle says you're the best."

Taylor hears Boyd Myers, but her thoughts are racing. Why is Isaiah with their client? She also hears Mr. Daniels' echo but is paralyzed with perplexity. She cannot comprehend why the handsome gentleman from the Mayor's Ball stands with her client. The lump in her throat handicaps her ability to speak. Recognizing she is blindsided to see him, Isaiah breaks the boundaries of her space and greets her with a hug. "Hello again, Counselor." In her mind, she faints.

She swiftly pulls from Isaiah's embrace. She felt the same electric shock wave she did when he hugged her at the Mayor's ball in Atlanta. "Hi," she musters. Suddenly, her brain comes back to life, and she quickly gathers herself. She greets Boyd, "Hello, Mr. Myers. It's nice to meet you. Are you ready to get started?"

Hansen and Mr. Daniels are baffled, so is Boyd. Peering back & forth between Isaiah and Taylor, Boyd asks, "Do you two know each other?"

Isaiah saves Taylor from her embarrassment. "Uncle introduced us at the Mayor's Ball on Saturday after I rescued her from the ledge." He lightens the mood.

Mr. Daniels and Hansen couldn't appreciate the humor. But Boyd bellows to Isaiah, "Man, this is..."

Isaiah abruptly intercepts Boyd's words. "Counselor, this is my brother, Boyd Myers."

Taylor acknowledges Isaiah's introduction. She exhales to clear her lethargy and turns to Hansen, "You're ready?"

Hansen is confused by what just happened but returns, "Yep."

"Let's do this," and Taylor walks to the summit—the crime scene. She submits to Boyd, "Walk us through what happened."

Boyd Myers shrugs his shoulders and says with the utmost confidence, "I can't."

"Why not?" She observes Boyd intently.

"Because I wasn't here," Boyd continues as if his life depends on it, and it does. "I did not shoot that detective—here or anywhere else."

"What do you mean here or anywhere else?" Taylor is taken aback by Boyd's insinuation of anywhere else.

Boyd pleads his innocence. "Ms. Alexander, there's no way that detective laid in this summit for as long as the media would have you believe. If the gunshot didn't kill him, his body would have singed. He would have burned to death."

"Burned to death?" The uncertainty on Taylor's face is plausible.

"Yes, burned to death. There was a forest fire out here the same week I am accused of shooting the detective. He would have cooked." Boyd looks keenly at Taylor, "Ms. Alexander, no one ever asked me—including you, to this point—but neither did I shoot nor did I have any involvement in the shooting of that detective. So I am sorry to waste your time coming out here, but I cannot tell you what happened because I wasn't here." The determination in Boyd's voice causes Taylor grave concern. No one bothered to interview him—not even his defense team.

Taylor asks Hansen, "Are you aware of this information?"

"Umm..." Hansen stumbles on his words. Boyd's explanation surprised him.

Non-accusingly, Taylor asks, "Mr. Myers, do you mind telling me where you were on the night in question?"

"Home." Boyd's cry is unnerving. It's the first time anyone listened to him.

"Alone?" Taylor pushes while the others observe in silence, but carefully listening.

Boyd continues persuading his innocence. "Yes. I returned from a long weekend in Maui. I ordered grub from Wacky Wok on the way home. The weekend activities and all the Mai Tai's influenced my soporific state. I ate and fell asleep on the couch."

Never taking her eyes off Boyd, Taylor asks the question, though it's meant for Hansen to verify. She bets no one checked with the restaurant. "Hansen, did we confirm this with the restaurant? It gives us a framework of time."

Encouraged she might fit one piece of this puzzle, "Mr. Myers, are there cameras installed in your building?"

"I believe so," Boyd reacts unsurely, and his flustered look is demonstrable.

"Hansen, we need the surveillance tapes if we don't already have them." She never turns to face Hansen, but hopes like hell he is taking this down. "Mr. Myers, is there anything else you'd like to tell me about that night—anything that may help prove your innocence?"

Boyd loosens up in his conversation with Taylor. He rubs his head as if to jog his memory, "I don't think so. As I said, I partied all weekend in Maui and was dead tired. I ate and fell asleep watching TV. I got up the next morning, did my usual—gym, shower, office."

"Anyone with you in Maui?" She glances at Isaiah from the corner of her eye. "Friends, relatives, girlfriend; anyone?"

"A few of my buddies," Boyd nervously answers Taylor. She wonders why. "Mr. Myers, are you associated with Detective Franklin at all?"

"No; I don't know the man."

"Thank you, Mr. Myers. That's all for now. We'll be in touch. And thank you for meeting us out here. I know it's unconventional." Boyd thanks Taylor before he and Isaiah start down the trail.

The surrounding activity bothers Taylor. A consistent flow of hikers occupied the trail. The summit is fenced but equally occupied by visitors. There are benches, tables, and a water fountain around the old buildings and restrooms. How could a body lie for three days and no one notice it? Mr. Boyd Myers' comment about the fire gave her a theory. As he indicated, if there was a brush fire, how could a body lying out here for three days remain intact? She needs the doctor's report to see if there was smoke inhalation? Burns? Carbon monoxide? Did the victim suffer any of these? The crime scene, as documented in the police report, does not match what she's observing. There is no report from the doctor on the victim. She couldn't even ask for a second sweep from forensics at this point. There is no investigator's report. Was the investigator's death connected to Detective Franklin's death? Why wasn't that investigation followed by her legal team? Why did they withhold details? And why didn't the Mayor mention the case—she couldn't shake that question?

When they reached the car at the peak, Mr. Daniels and Hansen got into her car. Apparently, they dismissed their driver. Taylor waits until they are on the 405 before she questions Mr. Daniels. "Are you going to level with me now, or do you want me to get on a plane back to Atlanta? Oh, let me guess. You're not at liberty to answer me."

"I shared with you what I could," Mr. Daniels maintains his disposition.

"Really. I'm trying a case on behalf of your firm, and you're not at liberty to share. That's just great! I'll call the Mayor and see if he's at liberty." The executive assistant answers, "Mayor's office," and Taylor retorts, "Taylor Alexander for Mayor Sellect, please."

"I am sorry, Ms. Alexander, he is not in the office at the moment. May I receive a message?"

"Yes, please have Mr. Mayor return my call." Without leaving her number, she hangs up. She figures if his nephew can find her home address to send her flowers, indeed the Mayor could find her cell number. And speaking of his nephew—that is, Mr. Isaiah Myers—she has no words. Nothing seems right about any of this.

Taylor could not concentrate when they returned to the office. A hike up Mt. Hollywood Peak will help to release her stress. She doesn't bother bringing work home; just tells Cathy to forward calls to her cell. While leaving, she runs into Mr. Daniels in the corridor. "Nice work today, Taylor."

"Thank you, sir, but I don't like being toyed with," Taylor snaps without breaking her stride.

"I'm sure you'll get that point across to Mayor Sellect." Mr. Daniel's words rang through the corridor.

"Good day, Mr. Daniels. I'll see you in the morning."

Taylor has no idea what to expect from this workout at Mt. Hollywood Park, but it excites her. When she joined the group, she read the distance is approximately 4.5 miles. Stone Mountain Park is five miles, so she should be okay. The difference is this is interval training, whereas Stone Mountain is cardio. Although everyone is at different fitness levels, the goal is to keep your heart rate elevated. Certain junctions are designated for resting and re-grouping. This workout will push her beyond her limits and give her a little friendly competition, guaranteeing her an elevated heart rate.

The group met at the Bronson Canyon Park entrance at 6:45 p.m. After warm-ups and introductions, they start the hike up Canyon Drive at 7:00 p.m. sharp and then on to the Bronson Caves. Taylor briefly explores the area before heading up a trail leading to the peak where there's a quick break to hydrate and enjoy the city view. After several winding paths, the final one heads down. This is one of the best workouts Taylor had in a long time. It was exhilarating, and she's glad she participated in the group.

When Taylor walks into the hotel's lobby, Isaiah, her client's brother, who is also the fine gentleman from the Mayor's ball, greets her. "May I have a word with you, Counselor?"

"You have 60 seconds... 59."

"I know you feel..." Isaiah starts, but Taylor cuts him off. "Oh, you've known me all of five minutes, but you know how I feel. This should be good."

Isaiah looks soothingly at Taylor and implores, "If you're only giving me 59 seconds, may I ask you not to interrupt, please?" Taylor did not allow herself to become hypnotized by his sensual voice. "And a smartass too. Wow!" She shakes her head, looking raptly at him; her frustration is noticeable.

Isaiah starts again, "Counselor, let me explain."

Unable to contain herself, Taylor cuts him off. "What is there to explain, Isaiah? I am sure you knew Mayor Sellect hand-picked me to try his nephew's case; yet failed to mention it to me—deliberately." She pauses, scrutinizing him.

"Honestly, I did not know until today. When Boyd asked me to ride with him, I figured he needed moral support. On the ride, he mentioned a bulldog attorney from Atlanta that Uncle hired for him. I thought it was a dude. Never in a million years did I think it was you."

Not letting his glistening puppy-dog eyes distract her, "And I'm supposed to believe you? Why?" Taylor is unashamed at revealing her irritation. If she is fair, it isn't all related to Isaiah, but he's standing in the line of fire.

"Because it's the truth; that's why." Isaiah stands helplessly, realizing she is not convinced. How would he convince her he had no idea she would be in Los Angeles, let alone the lead trial attorney on his brother's case?

"Okay. I believe you and your 60 seconds are up." Taylor's sarcasm cut through the air like a butcher's knife. And she didn't stop. "Would you please stop stalking me now?" She stomps toward the elevator, not allowing Isaiah to say anything else. He stands exasperated. How is he to make this right? While Isaiah contemplates, Taylor storms back into his presence. "May I see your cell phone, please?"

"Huh?" Isaiah is jumbled. Why does she want his phone?

Taylor knows her request is absurd. She also knows the Mayor wouldn't expect her on Isaiah's phone. He hadn't returned her call from earlier in the day, and she believes it's deliberate. "I would like to use your cell phone, please. May I?"

"Why?" He isn't in the habit of handing over his phone and not to someone he's known for, as she said, all of five minutes.

"Don't give it to me. But if you want me to believe you, dial Mayor Sellect." His uncle will kill him and bring him back to life, all in the same breath. But he needs her to believe him. He wants to know her, and already they are on the wrong foot. If calling his uncle makes it right, he'll endure the beating from his uncle. He dials the number and hands her the phone.

"Hey nephew," the Mayor answers. "Mr. Mayor, Taylor Alexander. Will you level with me, or shall I get on the first plane back to Atlanta?" Taylor's annoyance is outward. In his fatherly voice, the Mayor quiets Taylor.

"Now calm down, sweetheart. I said nothing because the less you know from me, the better you will try this case. The evidence will unfold. Just litigate the case." Mayor Sellect reassures Taylor.

"What are you keeping from me?" Taylor demands.

"Taylor, I am at a dinner meeting. I promise you my full attention in the morning. Tell my nephew he's a punk." The Mayor's attempt to lighten Taylor's mood is unsuccessful.

"I will be in your office at 10:00 a.m. tomorrow, Mr. Mayor." Taylor hands the phone to Isaiah and walks to the elevator.

"Hey, uncle."

Not giving Isaiah a chance to speak further, "You and I will talk later, nephew." And Isaiah heard a dial tone. He turns to address Taylor, but she is getting on the elevator. He walks to the revolving door and leaves the hotel defeated.

As she originally planned before her stalker met her in the lobby, Taylor relaxed in the Jacuzzi tub with a glass of Pinot Noir to rhythms that reduced her anxiety. Usually, she pipes hip-hop, but she needs soothing, relaxing sounds—not beats. The creator of this track and a sound therapist collaborated to mix fluid harmonies and gentle chimes to produce a rhythmic beat. This is exactly what she needs.

The workout was fantastic, but her body will hate her in the morning. After her Jacuzzi bath, she ordered the same Asian chicken salad she had when she arrived on day one and studied the remaining material in the file. She followed up on Boyd's suggestion of a brush fire during the time in question.

Taylor realizes she has neither checked on her youth center nor has she spoken to Dulaney. She knows Dulaney well enough to recognize she's processing her reactions to their one-sided conversation. When she is ready to talk, she'll call. But tomorrow, Taylor will call Coltrane to see how things are going at the Center. Right now, she will find that space between thoughts to retreat as she releases the stresses of the day. A knock on the suite's door disrupts her quiet time. It is room service with her salad. The timing is perfect because she is starved.

On Thursday morning, Taylor wakes refreshed and rejuvenated, although her muscles need a minute to forgive her for the workout the day before. She prepares for the day, remembering the idle thought she issued to the Mayor about being in his office at 10:00 a.m., and chuckles to herself. She arrives at the office just before 7:30 a.m. and settles into the conference room with her caramel macchiato.

First, she needs to make the connection between Mayor Sellect and the Judge. Who was the judge who granted bail? She'd gain insight from establishing that relationship. Every bit of information ordinarily found in discovery is missing. Where is the Application for Bail, and why isn't it in the file? Taylor doesn't bother asking Hansen. She goes to the Clerk's office and obtains a copy of the Order. She also gets a copy of the bail schedule. That will tell her if the judge deviated from the prescribed dollar amount for the crime for which Boyd Myers is charged. If the judge departed from the schedule, the reason is documented in the record.

Judge Randall Crane signed the Order granting bail and followed penal code section 187—attempted murder; bail set at $100,000. What is the Honorable Crane's relationship with Mayor Sellect? And to Boyd? None other than Isaiah Myers posted Boyd's bail. Taylor has to determine how to approach Isaiah. She doesn't know his financial state, so she doesn't presume he has $100K lying around. But first, she must figure out the relationship between the Mayor and the judge. Cathy informs Taylor when she returns that Mr. Daniels, Hansen, and Mayor Sellect are in the conference room.

Taylor slows her pace as she enters the conference room. "Good morning, gentlemen." The two older gents stand in unison, and the three men respond, "Good morning."

The Mayor addresses Taylor first. "Figured I'd help you make good on your idle threat by coming to you. You have my undivided attention for two hours. I must get back to Atlanta for an evening meeting."

Taylor's first instinct is to address the Mayor's comment regarding her threat. Instead, she dives in. "What is your relationship with the Honorable Randall Crane?"

"Crane and I go back."

"Do you care to elaborate?"

"We became friends on the lacrosse team in college, and our friendship grew over the years (or so I thought)." As Mayor Sellect recollects his friendship, the memories he and Crane shared on the lacrosse team; and then to his now wife (but Crane's then-girl) surface to the forefront of his mind.

His comment piques Taylor's interest. "What do you mean by so you thought?"

"Crane and I lost contact during law school. He came out here to the west coast, and I went southeast to Atlanta. I ran into Elaine at a social event the firm hosted for prospective law students. I first met Elaine on campus at school. We became friends, and now we're husband and wife. Unbeknownst to me, Crane dated Elaine when we were in college, but the relationship ended abruptly and on not-so-good terms. He's hated me ever since he learned we married."

"How does any of that factor into this case?" Hansen inserts.

"It's simple. Crane thinks I betrayed his friendship, and he's set Boyd up as payback." The Mayor is convinced of such a farfetched allegation.

"That's a pretty big allegation, Mr. Mayor." Taylor asserts.

"One I'll stake my life on." The Mayor is equally as stern, which quiets the room. Everyone ponders his or her thoughts.

Hansen breaks the silence. "But why kill a decorated detective?" His incomprehension is understandable.

"My research revealed Detective Franklin arrested Judge Crane at a rally when he was just out of law school. If the Mayor's theory has any validity, it means payback to Detective Franklin too." Taylor explains to Hansen. She knows this theory is a stretch, but she has no other, which reminds her to follow up on the fire Boyd mentioned.

"But what's Boyd's connection to Judge Crane?" Hansen asks.

"He has no direct connection that I am aware of. If Crane did his homework, he learned that Boyd is my nephew."

"Could they belong to the same gym? Country club? Anything?" Hansen digs deeper into possible connections between Boyd and Judge Crane.

"Boyd isn't the country-club type, so no. And I doubt Crane works out."

The lawyers conclude after rounds of discussion on the Mayor's revenge theory as the Mayor receives notice his car is en route. Taylor mentally notes Mr. Daniels didn't offer his opinion during the dialog. Her reflection is invaded when the Mayor leans to her ear as he leaves. "Go easy on my nephew. He is innocent." This information may be what she needs to engage in a conversation with Isaiah. After all, she wants to know details around his posting bail for Boyd.

These are serious allegations. Taylor wants to tread lightly but thoroughly. Pinning an attempted murder charge on an innocent man is not something the DA's office would risk. Taylor has no concrete evidence Boyd Myers committed the crime. In contrast, the DA's office has no proof he did. They need to verify every angle of his account of his whereabouts.

Taylor annotates the events leading to the crime and calls Isaiah. She is stunned when he answers on the first ring. "Hi. This is Taylor Alex..."

"Counselor, glad you called. Let me offer my profuse apologies for how this appears. I assure you, I am not a co-conspirator to my uncle's plan."

It is Taylor's turn to break in. "I know. He acquitted you this morning. Listen, I never thanked you for the flowers. I applaud your investigative skills, though. You tend to unveil where I lay my head, whether at home or in a hotel in a different city." Taylor smiles as she pesters Isaiah. "The flowers were beautiful. I also apologize for being rude the other day. I was overwhelmed when I saw you with your brother." Taylor is vulnerable.

"I am glad you enjoyed the flowers; I wasn't sure of your favorites. And no apology necessary, Counselor."

"Exotics are my second favorite."

"Duly noted. Did my uncle return your call this morning?" Isaiah continues with small talk. He doesn't want to end their call. "He will kill me for that stunt of yours."

"My stunt got his attention because he was in the office this morning." Taylor reverts to counselor mode. "And I asked him not to rough you up too badly." They share a laugh.

"Thanks, Counselor. I appreciate that. Is he still in town?"

Taylor doesn't contain her facetious. "You can track me like I am a shoelace attached to your oxfords, but you can't find your uncle." They cackle pretty hard.

Isaiah realizes Taylor isn't guarded. Encouraged, he steps into the moment. "Have dinner with me this evening?"

Isaiah catches Taylor off guard. "That is a very kind gesture, but..." He doesn't allow her to finish her rejection.

"Before you say no, think about it. You have to eat. Besides, you cannot work out in these hills without proper nourishment." Isaiah makes his case.

Taylor wonders if he is an investigator. How does he know she works out? "How did you...oh, yesterday—the workout?" Her memory served her as she recalls she was in workout gear when he stalked her in the lobby. "I'll think about it, Mr. Myers."

"That's all I ask. You have a lovely afternoon."

"You too." Taylor ends the call and dives into her search for facts surrounding Detective Franklin's shooting. She intentionally didn't ask Isaiah about posting bail during her conversation; she reserved that question for another time. Despite reviewing surveillance and medical records and creating scenarios connecting Boyd to Detective Franklin or Judge Crane, none of the pieces of this puzzle fit. Her only motive is the Mayor's dubious theory of revenge. That makes the Honorable Randall Crane her only suspect. Is he behind this crime? Judge Crane is an upstanding, law-abiding citizen who upholds the law.

Hansen and Taylor look up when Cathy taps on the door. She holds flowers, and a young lady dressed in white accompanies her. She has a table like those used by a hotel's room service. "This is Nina from Chaya. She is here to serve lunch."

"Cathy, we didn't order lunch." Taylor and Hansen look at each other, mystified.

"I know. Mr. Myers did." Cathy states.

Hansen blurts, "Cathy, we cannot accept lunch from Mr. Myers. He's the client." He looks to Taylor while Cathy places the flowers before her.

"Mr. Isaiah Myers. And these are for you, Taylor." Taylor reaches for the card. It reads, you never responded to my dinner invitation. I thought you forgot to eat. Bon appétit! Taylor shakes her head, amused. "Do you mind putting them on the side table? This one is covered in paper."

She and Hansen indulge in the delectable lunch courtesy of Isaiah Myers. Taylor prepares a serving for Cathy. Afterward, she calls Isaiah and thanks him for lunch. She was so consumed with the case; she forgot he asked her to dinner. Then she had a thought. "Cathy, will you Google Isaiah Myers and bring me the results, please?"

Cathy peers at Taylor inquisitively. "Looking for anything in particular?" She is glad Taylor asked about Isaiah. He called every day since seeing her at the crime scene. Cathy is optimistic Taylor is oblivious. Cathy searches, but she learned much of the basic stuff through conversations with Isaiah.

"The usual—profession, hobbies—you know, that kind of stuff."

A few minutes later, Cathy enters the conference room. Taylor and Hansen are eating lunch while buried in papers, black binders, and boxes. She hands Taylor a few sheets of paper from which she reads silently. Cathy stands quietly while Taylor reviews the information. Isaiah Monroe Myers, single, one daughter—8—Nyla, her mother is Lauren Jets, shares custody, a minority owner of the basketball team, biochemical engineer, owns his firm—Myers & Associates, works out at the private gym in the building he owns/lives in, shoots at the local range as a hobby, has specially packaged Cabernet Sauvignon sent to him from Sonoma County, not sure if he drinks or...

"Cathy, did you learn this from Google?" Taylor stops reading and looks in amazement at Cathy.

"Yes, and No. I ask him simple things when he calls. He's very polite and apologetic each time. As a thank you for my patience, he included my favorite dessert with your lunch today." Cathy explains to Taylor as Hansen listens in.

"I have no messages from him."

"He usually asks for your voicemail. You do check your voicemail, right?" Cathy returns a similar look to Taylor, who is in dismay.

She had not checked the office voicemail, ever. Her office is used primarily to store her handbag and client meetings. Most of her work takes place in the conference room. She has one client in Los Angeles and uses her cell phone to contact him, but most times, Cathy calls. Shaking her head to clear the sudden fog encapsulating her brain, Taylor thanks Cathy and goes back to her lunch.

"Did you hear your beau goes to the shooting range? Is your faith in him free of dubiety?" Hansen introduces skepticism into Isaiah's character.

"Are you suggesting he shot the detective?" Taylor is hesitant about this option. But she cannot dismiss it. Boyd is her client, and she must not leave any rock unturned in crafting his defense.

"I am suggesting we do our due diligence." Hansen returns to his lunch. Taylor loses her appetite. She is sickened by the notion. But they add the scenario to the puzzle, unrelentingly reviewing evidence. Neither realizes the time nor the horizon until Taylor's phone vibrates, alerting them to their surroundings.

She recognizes Isaiah's number, though not yet personalized in her contact list. Goosebumps rise on her arms as she answers. "Hello Counselor, this is your stalker. Are you still at the office?" Isaiah chuckles as he recalls Taylor calling him a stalker.

Taylor's heartstrings tug, it's a feeling she can't explain. She pushes Hansen's comment regarding the shooting range to the background of her mind. "Hi, stalker. Yes, I am still in the office."

"As I suspect. A car awaits downstairs. It's to take you to the restaurant of your choice (and you can bring your colleague with you). Option two is Nina delivers dinner as she did lunch." Taylor senses Isaiah's smile, and a girlish grin automatically paints her face.

"Why don't I propose option three?"

She rouses Isaiah's interest. "What is option three?"

Taylor cautiously flirts with Isaiah, eyeing Hansen, who light-heartedly listens to her conversation. "The waiting car drives me to a restaurant you choose in 45 minutes. You'll wait at the bar with my favorite glass of Cabernet Sauvignon."

Isaiah's mirth radiates through the phone. "I choose option three. See you in an hour, Counselor." He is overjoyed with option three. He only threw in "and you can bring your colleague" to influence Taylor to accept. The perfect place for wine comes to his mind—a classic neighborhood restaurant in Sonoma. They can relax in the sophisticated but casual bistro atmosphere and savor a silky Cabernet Sauvignon at the granite wine bar. But could Halé be prepared in an hour?

Taylor knows Hansen will give her a hard time. "Flirting with the client-emy; wait, that doesn't sound right?" Hansen pokes at Taylor, and they holler at his made-up word.

"No; it doesn't. And focus. We need to get to the bottom of this."

Hansen continues poking, "And we have 45 minutes until your big date." Taylor gives him a look, making him wonder if she is reverting to the person who ordered him around on day 1. They'd become comfortable with each other and found a cohesive working relationship.

"It's not a date. It's a glass of wine, Hansen." Although her voice is uncompromising, he hears a smile under her hard exterior. So he continues with his devilment.

"Whatever you say, Counselor." Hansen mimics Isaiah's voice. Taylor ignores him. After 55 minutes elapsed, Hansen reminds Taylor of her 45-minute commitment. "You are 10 minutes late for your date—I mean for your glass of wine." He pretends he misstated, knowing well what he said.

"Oh, snap!" Taylor blurts.

"Crackle and Pop." Hansen finishes Taylor's thought by impersonating the cereal slogan.

"That is not cute, Hansen. I'll take this file and review it tonight. Why don't you go home or go on a date? I'll feel bad if you stay here." Hansen saw beyond her tough façade to the lovely young lawyer who is fondly becoming his law companion.

"You mean you wouldn't enjoy your date while I am working?" Hansen torments and makes funny faces at Taylor from across the room.

She reminds him tastefully, "Truth be told, you should have completed this before now. So stay in your lane. Come on, let's get out of here."

Hansen and Taylor gather files to take home and head to their respective offices to retrieve their belongings, agreeing to meet at the elevator. When they reach outside, Taylor doesn't see a car. Before either she or Hansen says anything, Isaiah appears out of the blue. "Where did you come from? Where is your car?" Taylor questions.

"We don't need one. I'll explain when we get on the elevator." Isaiah takes Taylor's hand into his and leads her back into the building. Hansen is puzzled. He asks Taylor, "Everything all right, Counselor?" Is he calling her Counselor too? "Um, yes." Taylor is as bemused as Hansen. "See you in the morning."

"Okay; be careful," Hansen meets his ride who's sitting with the hazard lights flashing.

"Thank you, Hansen." Taylor and Isaiah disappear into the building where she spent the past 12 hours working. After they step into the elevator, Isaiah presses the button for the rooftop. Did he arrange for Nina to set up a candlelit dinner on the rooftop? Taylor stops in her tracks when she sees the helicopter on the helipad. Immediately, she remembers learning of the Emergency Helicopter Landing Facility code when she conducted research. It mandates each building have a rooftop emergency helicopter landing approved by the Fire Chief. She looks at Isaiah in awe. "Why do we need a helicopter to have a glass of wine?" Taylor yells above the loud engine.

"Because you said you want a glass of your favorite Cab, and there's only one place to get it," Taylor recalls Cathy's probing into Isaiah revealed he got his wine from Sonoma County. Is that where he's taking her? She wants to resist, and her mind supports her, but her feet did not receive or read the memo because they lead her to the helicopter. Isaiah helps her into the small cabin, strapping her in such that she can hardly breathe. After securing himself in the straps, he gives the pilot a signal that must mean take off. The helicopter lifts into the air. A bearable bumpy ride brings them to a field which is a landing zone, and a 5-minute car ride ends at the bistro.

The young woman greets Isaiah in a manner that causes Taylor to believe she knows him. "What's up, dude? How you been?" She wraps her long body around his muscular one.

"I am well. You must work on your grammar." Isaiah scolds the young lady who isn't bothered. "How are you?" He hugs her and plants a kiss on her cheek.

Embarrassed by Isaiah's actions, "Ugh! "I'm good." She wipes her cheek and jokingly punches him in his six-pack. "Is the lady why you called for the best Cab in the vineyard?" the young woman speaks low, but Taylor hears her. She grows uncomfortable as the two of them enjoy their exchange.

Isaiah beams as he looks at Taylor, "Yes; she is. Ms. Taylor Alexander, meet my adorable, sweet, baby cousin Amber." How many times did she tell him not to introduce her as his adorable baby cousin? He makes her sound like she is four years old; she's in college. Geez...

"Hello, Amber. It's nice to make your acquaintance." Amber whispers to Isaiah, "Is she uppity? Or does she just talk proper?" Taylor wonders if Amber believes she is invisible; obviously, she can hear her whisper, which isn't a whisper at all.

Isaiah pretends to whisper back to Amber. "I will take you over my lap. Now behave."

Amber knows Isaiah is serious. He is fun, but he is also big on proper etiquette. Amber apologizes to Taylor, "I'm sorry, Miss." Addressing Isaiah, who knows his way around the bistro, "Do you need me to show you, or you'll make your way?"

"I sure hope you don't treat all your patrons this way." And he led Taylor to the granite wine bar where they awaited a bottle of Hughes Wellman 2007 Cabernet. This wine has an opaque purple/black color. Its blackberry essence is woven with mocha, graphite, and Crème de Cassis. Its blueberry fruit, black raspberry, and crushed plum make this fine wine mouthwatering and dense. For the wine lover, its finish is a sixty-second experience not to be missed—a succulent combined taste of Cabernet Sauvignon, Petite Verdot, and Merlot.

This is, by far, the best Cab she ever tasted. After the trial, she will stay an extra day or two to visit the vineyard. She'd get Dulaney to join her. Speaking of Dulaney, not only hasn't she talked to her, she hasn't sent Taylor's clothes. She is coming to the end of her limited clothing supply.

Isaiah inquires. "Like? Dislike? Up in the air?"

"Love it! I don't know if it's the blackberry or the black raspberry that gives it the distinction, but I love it. This is a perfect end to a very long day. And thank you for lunch. That was kind of you." Taylor guardedly treasured the handsome man sitting across from her as he smiles at her. That damn smile is intoxicating.

"It's my pleasure. I know you are not eating well, given the long hours in the office. I will do it every day if you will allow it." The look in his eyes and the tone of his voice confirm he is serious. So she jokes, "Don't bite off more than you can chew."

Isaiah flirts. "Oh, I have a very hefty appetite, Counselor." Taylor doesn't respond. She does not want to take this conversation to a place of no return. Given that, she shifts the conversation. "Do you mind if we order tapas? I haven't eaten…"

Isaiah finishes her sentence, "…since I fed you lunch."

"You didn't feed me lunch. You provided me with lunch." Taylor doesn't allow him to play on words.

"But I would feed you and enjoy every minute," the words flow off his tongue as smooth as a cool breeze. Again, Taylor doesn't want to take the conversation somewhere she can't come back from. She ignores Isaiah's comment and asks, "May we get menus, please?"

"Come. I requested a table." Isaiah helps Taylor off the stool, picks up her glass of wine, and escorts her to a table in the back corner of the bistro. The table is dressed with small plates of curried cashews, oysters on the half shell, a marinated mix of something, French onion soup, and French fries. Isaiah pulls out a chair for Taylor. After she sits, he softly slides it under the table, taking his seat next to her.

She asks, "What's with the French fries?"

"I heard you are a French fry junkie. But try the curried cashews with your wine first." Did Cathy tell him she loves French fries? Maybe he learned it from the Mayor. She did as she is told and is gratified. The curry taste from the cashew with the wine is a perfect blend. She isn't an oyster fan, so she tries the French onion soup and eats all of it. She nibbles on the curried cashews with her second glass of wine. Much to her amazement—and his—she hardly touches her fries. She and Isaiah are engrossed in their conversation; they don't notice the bistro closed. The owners are friends, so they don't bother him. But he respects other's time, so he pays the wait staff, hugs his nosey cousin good night, and leads Taylor out of the bistro to the car. In the 5-minute ride to the helicopter, Taylor nods.

When they are back at the helipad, Isaiah does not want to wake her. He admires her. Sexy. She's too damn sexy—even in her sleep. She must be tired to sleep on the bumpy ride. How he'd love to carry her to the bed, undress her, and have his way with her body. He nudges her out of her peaceful place. "How long was I… Did I sleep the entire day?" Isaiah softly places his index finger over her lips and says, "It's okay. Let's get you to the hotel." He helps her out of Halé and takes the short walk to the hotel with her. At her suite door, he cautiously kisses her on her forehead and says, "Goodnight, Counselor." His mind takes a field trip on all the ways and all the things he wants to do with her.

"Thank you for the perfect end to a long day. And thank you again for lunch." Taylor appreciates Isaiah.

"You are welcome. Get inside and get some sleep. May I call you tomorrow?"

"Yes; you may. Goodnight." Taylor steps into the suite, closes the door, and crawls under the covers, half-dressed. She slept peacefully.

CHAPTER 3

Trial Prep

It's Friday morning; Taylor scheduled a prep session with Boyd. She didn't include him on her initial witness list filed with the Court, but she can supplement the list. Her decision to call him as a witness rests mainly on his testimony; it must be flawless.

Boyd is on trial for the attempted murder of Detective Franklin, a decorated LAPD officer, but the prosecution has no principal evidence connecting him to the crime or the victim. There's no concrete evidence substantiating the cause of the act, but it is fair to infer it was a brutal shooting. The allegations are the assailant shot the victim and dumped him at the Santa Monica Mountains' top. However, the defendant is known amongst friends, family, and the community as a peaceful man—engaged in serving his community. This might have a bearing in the minds of the jury. Could a man of his character shoot a police officer and leave him in the mountains to die?

Taylor established no connection between the Honorable Randall Crane and the DA's office. She uncovered nothing in her research indicating corruption or criminal connections. It's mindboggling to consider Judge Crane's involvement in this crime and the abuse of his authority to carry it out. There must be a theory other than revenge, a believable one that she proves and the jury believes.

Cathy peeks in the conference room as Taylor preps for Boyd, who's in the waiting area. Cathy's unusualness stops Taylor in her tracks. "Ms. Alexander…"

"Please call me Taylor, Cathy." The ladies spoke many times about the formality, but Cathy insists on calling her Ms. Alexander.

She flinches, "Sorry; it's a habit. But Taylor"—they laugh at Cathy's awkwardness in calling her Taylor—"there's a lady in the waiting area who says she is your stylist." Taylor's wide-eyed look causes Cathy's look of wonder.

"I don't have a stylist." Taylor's puzzled look grows with confusion. Cathy deemed this to be another one of Isaiah's surprises, though he didn't mention it.

"You don't? Do you think Mr. Myers sent her?"

Taylor stood attentively, eyes bucking, "I will shoot him between his ears (without killing him) if he did. Send her in quickly; let's see what she says. Besides, I might need her. My best friend was supposed to send clothes from my closet, but I don't yet have them." Taylor makes a mental note to call Dulaney this weekend. "Oh, and tell Boyd I'm delayed."

Shortly after Cathy left the room, the stylist taps on the door. "Ms. Alexander?" Wow, her makeup is flawless—it's the first thing Taylor notices, complimented by a chic short hairstyle with diamond studs sparkling from each ear. She wears a simple but stunning dark purple belted dress adorned with multi-colored pumps. She has no handbag, only a phone, cardholder, and something unrecognizable in her hand.

"Hi. Please call me Taylor," gesturing for her to enter. If anyone is to style her, this lady is the one. She is stunning, girly, but not over the top, and sexy but gracious. "How can I help you?"

Exuding contagious confidence as she steps into the conference room, "Thank you, Taylor. I am here to get your measurements." She holds a tape measure in her hand. "I am hired to purchase five of the hottest, unique navy blue attire there are in Los Angeles," she reads from her phone. "They are to be classic but posh. Sharp, but chic. Powerful, but lady-like."

Taylor is curious. "May I ask who hired you?"

The stylist isn't sure if it's curiosity or concern she observes on Taylor's face. "Ms. Dulaney Smith hired me," easing Taylor's interest. "She said if I did not carry out her prescribed orders, she wouldn't have a best friend on Monday." Again, reciting from her phone. This time she smiles when she finishes reading.

Taylor is relieved Dulaney sent the stylist and not Isaiah. She recalls her brief comment about her wardrobe the night he took her to Sonoma for a glass of wine. "Did she give you a script?" The ladies explode in laughter, and the stylist places her phone on the table.

Stepping to Taylor with her tape measure expanded, the stylist assesses Taylor. "Let me confirm your measurements. You look to be a size six, maybe a four, but let me measure to be exact." The tape measure is around Taylor's hips; she stands stationary. "Ms. Smith said you have an impending trial, and you need clothing."

"Yes, Ms. Smith is correct." Taylor speculates why Dulaney sent a stylist instead of suits from her closet. Her body shifts when she transfers her weight from one leg to another, causing the stylist to pause.

"Okay, Ms. Alexander. I have what I need," she steps back, allowing space between her and Taylor, and presses a button on her tape measure to close it. "I will deliver the suits to your hotel later today," she enters Taylor's measurements in her phone. "Will a classic navy pump suffice?"

Taylor responds while the stylist packs to leave. "Yes, a classic navy pump and a sexy strap stiletto."

The ladies move toward the door to exit, and Taylor adds, "I'll have Cathy provide you with my credit card."

"Ms. Smith took care of the costs." She hands Taylor her business card. "If you have any issues with the pieces, please do call." Wait. Did she say Dulaney paid her? Dulaney is thrifty and does not spend money if the purchase has nothing to do with music equipment or her stage costumes. Maybe she considers the suits Taylor's stage costumes for the courtroom.

Taylor takes the stylist's business card, extends her gratitude, and walks her out. She acknowledges Boyd, who is waiting in the reception area. He is typing on his phone. "I am so sorry to keep you waiting. Come on back." They proceed down the hallway to her office. File boxes and papers plaster the conference room, making it unsuitable for a client meeting.

Taylor and Boyd enter her office and take their seats. No sooner than they're seated, Taylor's cell phone vibrates. Pointing to her phone, she asks Boyd, "Do you mind if I take this—just one minute?" Boyd agrees to her request. Taylor isn't sure if Boyd noticed his brother's number on her phone screen, but she answers, "Hi," and walks a few feet to the window. In a quieter voice, "I would love to talk to you, but I have another Mr. Myers in my office, and he's been waiting a while. May I return your call?"

Smiling on the other end of the conversation at how lightly Taylor is speaking, Isaiah teases, "Which Mr. Myers is more handsome?"

Following suit, Taylor responds with a bit of sassiness, "I don't know, but we can debate when I return your call. Bye." She smiles inwardly as reflections of Isaiah in the black tux at the Mayor's ball in Atlanta come to memory. He is the more handsome brother.

Taylor walks back to the chair and apologizes for the disruption. Boyd emboldens her. "If your interruption puts a smile on your face like the one you're wearing, then it's well worth the wait."

Feeling her face turn red with embarrassment, Taylor asks, "Are all you Myers' men full of..." she catches herself. This is her client. To complete that question is uncouth, despite her connection to his uncle, the Mayor. "Where were we, Mr. Myers," she again takes her seat next to him.

"Aren't you going to finish your question?" Boyd pokes at her. He assumed it was his brother whose call she accepted—at least for his brother's sake. He hoped it was him.

"No, I am not." Taylor messes with the papers she picked up off the desk to avoid looking his way. Not only is it unprofessional, but it is also inappropriate to finish that question to her client.

"I will answer it anyway." Boyd didn't let it rest. "Yes, we are all full of crap, and we'll charm our way out of anything." Taylor wants to ask, will you charm your way out of this attempted murder charge, but that would be highly incongruous.

Dismissing Boyd Meyers' comment, Taylor refocuses the conversation. "I'd prefer to go to the courthouse to simulate what happens if you take the stand. I'll act as the prosecutor; Hansen, the defense attorney." Taylor ensures Boyd's attention shifts with the conversation and no longer smirks at her. He's focused, so she continues. "That way, you'll get a feel for what happens should you take the stand. Good?" She pauses again in case Boyd needs to clarify or ask a question. He shakes his head, so Taylor continues explaining. "We'll focus primarily on rebuttal testimony to get you comfortable with the prosecutor's tactics when questioning you."

Again Boyd Myers agrees, "Good."

Taylor is in full-on attorney mode. She stands and places the papers on the desk, turns to Boyd, and asks, "Questions?"

"Yes, one." Boyd rubs his hands together as if examining his question.

Taylor leans against the mahogany desk, resting her hands on each side of her for support, "Go ahead." She looks at Boyd intently as he continues rubbing his hands, faster and nervously. "What determines if you put me on the stand?" He manages, and as he does, he unconsciously slows the rubbing of his hands, almost to a halt.

"Truthfully, I don't know yet. Instinct." Taylor's position on the desk remains, but she pulls one leg in for balance as she notices Boyd's agitation grows. The lines on his brow creases, and he bites his bottom lip. Without speaking, he rises and paces a small area of the office near his chair. He slows his pacing, places both hands on the back of the chair where he was seated, leans over the chair, and asks Taylor in a deliberate tone. "You do realize my life is on the line, don't you? And you're operating on instinct?"

He does not wait for an answer but paces the same as he did a few seconds ago. His breath is pulsating. Once again, he takes the same position on the back of the chair and in the same tone, "Lady, have you lost your everlasting mind?" Boyd is beyond agitated.

Taylor shifts her position on the desk. Calmly, she reassures Boyd, "Mr. Myers, there are several factors involved. We'll evaluate them as the trial progresses and decide when, or if, it comes to that. My instinct will guide me." Taylor examines Boyd's disposition to determine if her words ease his anxiety before she continues. She walks in Boyd's direction and pleads with him. "Trust that I know what I am doing. If you do not trust me, I can move to withdraw as counsel and ask for a continuance to provide you time to find a new lawyer." Taylor is empathetic with Boyd, but defending a black man who allegedly shot a police officer is a weight in and of itself. White police officers have a blank check when it comes to self-defense. However, the system does not favor black men the same. And she is tasked with trusting that same system—one in which she took an oath. Despite her faith in the judicial system, she knows the uphill battle she faces. Considering all, she cannot defend him if he doesn't trust her.

Boyd leans on the back of the chair, deflated. "Can I have a minute to talk to my brother and my uncle?" He sits, drops his head into the palms of his hands, and forces the air out of his lungs. Taylor understands his fear.

Again she reassures him. "Absolutely, but it is not your brother nor your uncle on trial. You must trust me, not them." Taylor places her hand on the back of Boyd's right shoulder to comfort him before she walks out of the office, giving him time to consult his family.

She walks down the corridor and settles in a phone room. As she dials Dulaney, her phone lights to an incoming call from Isaiah. Her initial reaction is not to answer and continue her call. But she aborts her call and answers, "Hello."

"Is everything okay?" He asks such that it stirs Taylor.

"Sure. Why do you ask?" It was only a short while since she told him she'd return his call. They ended their call jokingly, but his tone now is disturbing.

"One, Boyd called me frantic, and two, you did not answer with your usual Mr. Meyers." Taylor hears the concern in Isaiah's voice.

She empathized with Boyd. He faces serious allegations, and while his uncle finances his defense, it isn't apparent he has moral support. Taylor comforts Isaiah. "Boyd's reaction is normal—partly nervous, partly scared."

Isaiah isn't reassured; he is exasperated. "Do you think your scare tactic is effective? He said you told him he has to find a new lawyer."

Taylor did not like Isaiah's tone, nor did she appreciate his insinuation. "I do not have, nor do I need scare tactics," the lawyer in her surfaced. "And, that is not what I told him. Maybe you should be with him for moral support."

Isaiah realizes his comment doesn't sit well with Taylor. He adjusts his tone and asks, "Do you mind telling me what you said to him?"

Taylor powerfully addresses him. "Yes, I do mind, but I will tell you, anyway. What I said is if he doesn't trust me to do what's best for him, then I will ask for a continuance to allow him time to find new counsel." Boyd missed her point, which is he needs to trust her, not his uncle or brother. If someone he trusts could and would better serve him, then she wants that for him.

Isaiah pushed an unfamiliar button on Taylor. "Whoa, Counselor. Calm down." He'd explore another time. He wants to support his brother. "I am on my way to your office. I'll hold Boyd's hand if you believe that's what he needs."

Taylor's thoughts collide in her mind. What does he mean if I deem that's what Boyd needs? His brother is accused of attempted murder? Is it not commonplace that moral support from family is vital? "Why do I have to tell you that? Your brother faces attempted murder charges. Your uncle writes checks, and I'm not sure what you do, but he's always in this office alone. Do you realize the depth of the allegations? I am good at what I do, and I will work the soles off my stilettos, but he needs one of you, both of you. I don't know why I have to tell you." It saddens Taylor she must influence Isaiah to support his brother.

He loses points with Taylor. Family is important to her. He is lackadaisical with his brother, who may go to jail for a very long time. His lack of support of Boyd turns her off somewhat. Why should she become involved with a man who doesn't fully back his family? Is this what she expects from him?

"This is your brother. Why aren't you here for him? He is an emotional wreck."

Isaiah hears the cry in Taylor's plea. She is right; he isn't accompanying Boyd as he should. "I am doing what I can. There are things you don't know, so don't condemn."

"Sounds like you are judging yourself."

"Taylor, let's not go to war with each other. I am approaching your building. Will you come to the lobby for a second, please?" Isaiah wants to see her before she preps Boyd. The tension is unnerving in this conversation. He needs to safeguard her impression of him. Then he will walk with Boyd through his ordeal. He isn't sure he can provide the emotional support Boyd needs, but he will show up.

"Why do you want me to come to the lobby?"

"Will you come down, Counselor? Five minutes is all I ask."

"Isaiah, we need to get to the courthouse to prep Boyd for the stand. Can't it wait?" Taylor is exhausted with this exchange.

Isaiah insists. "No, Counselor, it cannot wait. Boyd will get what he needs, but I need to see you first. Come downstairs, please." Taylor doesn't speak but exits the phone room toward the elevator. Because she doesn't end the call, Isaiah hears her movement. When the elevator stops on the lobby level and opens, she makes one step to exit and bumps into Isaiah. He stands in the middle of the entry and exit point. She steps back while he enters the elevator. He wraps his arms around her waist and gives her a sweet hug. The elevator door closes, but it doesn't move as either press the number to her floor. He presses the number and says, "It sounded to me like you needed a hug. Now let's get Boyd calmed." Neither said anything else on the elevator ride.

When the elevator reaches the 25th floor, Isaiah speaks. "Ready, Counselor?" Taylor answers with a sharp, "Yes, I am ready." And they go to her office, where Boyd is on the phone.

"Whose that?" Isaiah interrupts Boyd's conversation.

"Uncle." Before Boyd says anything else, Isaiah takes the phone and speaks into it, "Uncle, I got this. We'll call you later."

"Thank God you are there. Talk to you later, nephew."

After several hours of trial preparation, everyone—Hansen, Boyd, Taylor, and Isaiah—is mentally drained. Boyd impressed Taylor with his testimony. He is equipped to take the stand, if necessary.

It's now late Friday afternoon. She and Hansen must recap, fill in a few loose ends, and then she'll treat Hansen to dinner. He never talks about dating, despite teasing her, but she will get into his business at dinner. Taylor said to everyone as she stuffs her bag with papers, "Okay, gentlemen. I think we're good."

"After all that, you think?" Boyd can't help himself. He felt like an 18-wheeler ran him over, a lion ate him alive, and someone beat him with an iron rod.

"You did well." Taylor encourages him. "Hansen and I will head back to the office to wrap up. If we have last-minute questions, we'll call you. Otherwise, we will talk with you next week."

Witnessing Taylor as the prosecutor and Hansen as the defense attorney during their trial simulation this afternoon, Boyd is pleased they are his legal team. He is confident they will prove his innocence. "Thank you, Ms. Alexander. I trust you." Boyd is humbled.

"That's good to know, Mr. Myers." Taylor gives Boyd a comforting smile.

"Any woman who will work the soles off her red bottoms is trustworthy to me." She is shocked Isaiah told his brother what she said. During their conversation, she conveyed the importance of moral support to Isaiah, and she told him she would work the soles off her stilettos for her clients.

"I am glad to know you can appreciate a fine pair of shoes, Boyd Myers," Taylor responds without looking at him, but instead, looks candidly at Isaiah and winks. With that, she places her crossover on her shoulder, and she and Hansen head out of the courtroom.

"Counselor, may I have a word with you?" Isaiah diverts her.

"Depends on whether that word stays between us or if you'll disperse it like cash from an ATM." Taylor can't help herself but giggles as she retorts those words at Isaiah. Her smile comforts him, but he isn't wholly relieved.

It wasn't his intent to break Taylor's trust by sharing their conversation with Boyd. He shared it to get him to see she is working on his behalf, and she would do what is necessary—within legal bounds—to prove he did not shoot the detective. "Understand Boyd is a ladies' man. Using the shoe analogy is a language he understands. I promise to make it up to you." Isaiah pleads for mercy. "I'll even buy you a pair of red bottoms."

Taylor isn't troubled because he shared their conversation; she is surprised. However, since he offered a pair of shoes, she listens. Everyone who knows her will attest to her shoe craze. "Now you've got my attention. Size 8.5M," Taylor is eye-to-eye with Isaiah.

"Not an issue, Counselor." She knows by his look he is genuine. "I'm going to spend time with my brother this evening; you know, keep him relaxed. We'll likely grab a few beers and shoot a few games of pool." Isaiah gives Taylor details of his evening, and she is both flattered and stunned. "Will you do me a favor and leave the office before 7:00

p.m. and relax? I sent a bottle of your favorite Cabernet Sauvignon to the hotel for you."

"How kind of you. I appreciate it."

Isaiah worked up the courage to make his request, and he hopes she is open to it. "I'd like it if you allow me to join you on your workout excursion tomorrow. We can get breakfast afterward."

Taylor admits to herself she is growing fond of Isaiah. If she were honest, she'd realize she smells the lingering scent of his cologne and the after-effects of his touch. She sometimes dreams of how his mouth tastes against hers. She didn't plan to work out in the morning, but his appeal caused her to consider. "I plan to sleep late tomorrow, get a massage, and catch up on happenings at the Foundation. But..."

Isaiah doesn't give her a chance to say no. He wants to spend time with her, and the specific activities do not sway him. So he offers, "You sleep in, have a late breakfast, and handle your work for the Foundation. If you are up to it later, we'll take a hike and get some grub." Nowhere in his suggestion is her massage. Isaiah notices her wheels spinning. He isn't sure she's okay having a massage with him, but he suggests. "Then we'll get massages. I'll arrange for the spa." He is poised, so he builds on his proposal. "Afterwards, join me at my spot for a movie and relaxation. Or, we can watch the movie in your suite—whichever you're comfortable with. The only thing you can ditch is the hike."

Taylor is intrigued. She wants to get to know him, but she won't make it obvious to him. "I'll call you, Mr. Myers, and let you know. But it sounds good." Her smile is sufficient for Isaiah. "I promised to take Hansen to dinner this evening. We need to get to the office to wrap up. You boys have fun!"

While Taylor and Isaiah discuss their plans for Saturday, Hansen went to the Clerk's office. The young lady who assists him is a cutie, so Hansen flirts with her. He's noticed her on other occasions when he filed pleadings but never interacted with her socially. The two steps into the corridor and engage in flirtatious conversation, causing Hansen to invite her to dinner. She accepts. Hansen thought Taylor wouldn't be the only one on a date tonight. He assumes Taylor and Isaiah are planning dinner. When Taylor approaches Hansen, she slows, gently placing her hand on his shoulder, and informs him, "I'll wait for you outside."

"I'm coming," Hansen turns to the cutie and says, "I'll see you at 8:30 p.m."

Taylor isn't sure she heard him right. When he catches up to her, she asks, "Did you just say see you at 8:30 p.m.?"

"Yes, I have a date too." Hansen pokes Taylor on her shoulder with his finger.

Stopping in her tracks and looking at Hansen befuddled. "Too? Silly, I was taking you to dinner tonight to thank you for working from sunup to sundown these past several weeks." Hansen looks to Taylor, speechless. She smirks at him. "But I'm glad you have a date. I can't wait to hear all about it." Taylor and Hansen walk back to the skyscraper. By the time they tie up loose ends, it is 7:15 p.m. Hansen hurries home to prepare for his date. Taylor takes a slow walk to the hotel, looking forward to a glass of the fine wine awaiting her.

The morning sun blitzes its way through the windows in Taylor's suite—radiant and full of life. It is 7:35 a.m. She intends to sleep in, but her stomach growls. She slides her feet into her slippers and retrieves the bowl of fruit from the fridge. Sitting on the bed, determined to get back in it, she tunes her iPod to a devotion playlist and worships as she indulges in the fruit. After her talk with God, she crawls under the covers and drifts back to sleep—the songs hum in her ears. When she wakes again, it is 11:05 a.m. "Sweet Jesus, I didn't intend to sleep all morning," Taylor mumbles, rubbing her eyes to clarify the time.

After showering, she dresses in her last pair of clean sweats and a tank top. Her late breakfast arrives from room service as she pulls the tank over her head. She motions the young woman to the small counter where she ate her eggs, turkey sausage, and toast while reading the paper. After breakfast, she has two items on her agenda—call Coltrane and call Dulaney.

Taylor's phone alerts her to a missed call from Coltrane. "Siri, call Trane."

"I'll be damned. If not for the updates of your trial on TV, I would've thought you abandoned us. This place could have burned to the ground. Who leaves home and doesn't check on their children, young lady?" Coltrane's greeting met Taylor with a burst of laughter.

"Hello to you too! Since I left my children in the most capable, caring hands, there's nothing to worry about." Taylor butters up to Coltrane, who's graciously operating her Foundation while she is in Los Angeles.

"If memory serves me, I am the second most capable." Coltrane reminds Taylor she believes Dulaney is most capable; he is just the most available.

"Okay, okay. I concede." He is never going to me live that down. "Are you treating my children well?" Two weeks is the most time Taylor's ever left the Center. She trusts Coltrane, but that place is her heart and soul.

"All's well, Ms. Alexander. I am having the time of my life with your badass kids." Coltrane assures Taylor. And it's true; he has a blast with the youth at her Center. The way she showers the kids with love and compassion causes you to wonder if she birthed them. Coltrane has a renewed opinion for Taylor's commitment to the Center.

"They are not bad, Trane. They merely need guidance and discipline." Taylor isn't sure why she defends the youth to Coltrane; she is preaching to the choir.

"Oh, and discipline they now know." Coltrane kids. Knowing she'll react to his next comment, he continues, "I will teach you how to discipline them upon your return. You know—so both the parent and the guardian rear in the same manner." Laughing and switching topics before Taylor replies, Coltrane asks, "How's it going out there?"

Recognizing his suave detour, "Don't think for one second I do not comprehend your co-parenting remark. What are you doing to my children?" Taylor did not consent to the diversion.

Coltrane knows all too well how passionate she is about the youth at her Center, so he convinces her. "They are just fine. And both children and guardians are having a blast." Taylor heeds the joy in his tone as he shares recent activities. "I took the boys to Dave & Buster's yesterday. I promised the girls I'd take them skating today. I'm reviewing permission slips as we speak." Coltrane's affection and interest in the youth's wellbeing in his short tenure are palpable, which warms Taylor's heart. "Chill... I got this. I'm also planning a fundraiser because you need new computers, kiddo. The kids are helping." Although Taylor has no details on this fundraising event, she is moved that her youth touched Coltrane's spirit. He continues, "You worry about your trial and not us. We're good."

She thanks him, "Don't get too comfortable in my chair, Dude. I am listening for the reason for field trips, and I want to hear about this fundraiser." Coltrane relaxes in the chair, props his feet on the desk, and explains.

"The first week, they agonized over your absence. I deviated from your plan because I appreciated and understood their emotions." Taylor abruptly intrudes, "Coltrane, you cannot deviate from…"

Stopping her mid-sentence to ease her rising pressure, "Hold on, hold on. I challenged them to write a 300-word essay explaining why they miss you, and the impact—negative or positive—your absence has on them, whether that includes school, home, social, whatever." Coltrane gauges Taylor's demeanor. She's composed, he continues. "Your spoiled brat (as the others call him), Kevin, wanted to know what's in it for them. Dave & Busters and Golden Glide field trips are their rewards." Tearing up as he recalls sentiments from the youth's papers, "Tay, when you read their essays, you will be in awe. You have a profound impact on their lives. I understand why you chose the Foundation over the role of CEO of the conglomerate."

Tears formed behind Coltrane's comments. It wasn't easy to forgo her role as CEO of her father's firm, but she knows it was the right thing to do in her soul. Coltrane continues to share the events of the past weeks. "I bought them junk food last week and told them it was from you because you missed them. Kevin wanted proof—adamant that he wasn't breaking the rules because you rarely serve junk food."

"Did he?" She misses her kids. She hopes they understand she takes work to fund the Center. She explained to them when she accepted the case and encouraged them to stay on their individual courses.

"Yep. Your secretary told me it's something you occasionally do." Hearing the softness in Taylor's voice, Coltrane shifts the conversation. If he shares any more, she will cry uncontrollably. "Listen, I don't want to interfere in your trial—hell, if you're not prepared now (Coltrane laughs)—but I need you to review the draft proposal. I will send it to commercial computer companies, asking them to donate computers to the Foundation, but I need your signature." Coltrane is absorbed in adding value to Taylor's center to help enrich those youths' lives in a short time. They inspire him. "My firm will donate two, and I'll reach out to a few homies." Coltrane couldn't comprehend why Taylor never asked them to donate computers. She has dinosaurs in the center. "The initial goal is 15." Coltrane is infected by the need to help her youth after spending only a few weeks with them. That touches Taylor's heart.

"Thank you, Trane, for having an interest and for caring. I cannot express how ecstatic I am to hear you excited about the only thing that matters to me." Taylor is motivated as she discusses the proposal with Coltrane. She will solicit donations from firms as well. She is ecstatic to replace the old computers. They didn't discuss the fundraiser, but she would use the funds to upgrade the servers and complete renovations. Her vision for a technology-driven, innovative Center for the inner-city youth is coming to life.

"Thank you, Tay, for entrusting your most prized possession to me. It's given me a new perspective in this short time." Coltrane is influenced to change his firm. His organization can do more than recruit talent, but once on board, he would ensure the young black talent is educated on the industry and gain coaching on life skills and financial planning and management. These slight changes would prove monumental in his clients' lives.

"Taylor, why haven't you done this before today? You know heavy hitters; we both do. These kids can be prepared to compete on the same level as every other child in the world." Drive, a little encouragement, and support are what they need.

Taylor recounts the day she deferred her role as CEO of the family's firm to focus on her passion. "It is the very reason I do it. Somebody pushed me. I recall Dad feeding college students, giving them a ride, and Sunday dinner. He bought books; students came to the office—never met him—and his secretary distributed them. I want to carry out that legacy. Not to mention the joy on the kids' faces and the light in their eyes when they sense someone cares. That is enough for me. I'd trade every pair of red bottoms to see that joy on each of their faces.

In true Coltrane fashion, "You can trade a pair of red bottoms for a computer." Coltrane and Taylor burst into laughter.

"Thank you; really, thank you. I appreciate what you're doing. Send the proposal to me. I'll review it while you are falling on your tail at Golden Glide—you never learned how to skate." They snicker, and Coltrane quickly dismisses the memory of his and Dulaney's first date at the skating rink. Taylor intrudes on his thoughts as she shifts into Mom-mode, "Ann needs moral support; she's shy. If you haven't, solicit female chaperones. You can handle the boys; girls are different creatures. We are emotional and need attention. You boys are not."

Coltrane was reminded more times than he cares to remember that Men are from Mars. "I am painfully aware. But we can't live without y'all." Just then, Chantal peeks into the office where Coltrane sits behind the desk which is hardly a desk but a sleek table. "Mr. Coltrane, if you need help with the girls today, I am here."

Bantering Taylor as he motions her secretary into Taylor's office, "See how dedicated we are while you're away playing in Los Angeles." Coltrane presses the speaker button and places his phone atop the desk so Taylor can say Hi.

"Hello, Cheney. Thank you for helping Mr. Coltrane while I am playing in LA." Taylor's mischievous laugh mocking Coltrane comes through the speakerphone. Taylor values Cheney; she is a bright young lady who aspires to work in the juvenile justice system. When she began, she volunteered one day a week and as her school schedule allows. Currently, she's at the Center almost every day the door opens.

"Ms. Alexander!" the excitement in Cheney's voice is apparent. "Hi! Ooohhh, Ms. Alexander, you will love how Mr. Coltrane changed your office. It's spacious like this. And…"

Taylor interjects in Cheney's excitement, describing changes to her office. "Did you say change…" Cheney gasps, shaking her head at Coltrane while she whispers, "You didn't tell her?" Cheney and Coltrane eye each other, pointing at the phone as if their hands are caught in the cookie jar.

"I can hear you, Cheney; it's on speaker."

Looking for a grand escape from Taylor's interrogation, Coltrane stands and says, "Would you look at the time. We must prepare for the skating rink. Ms. Alexander, we'll e-mail the proposal and follow up later. Okay." All three laugh. It is clear Coltrane doesn't want to address Cheney's oops moment.

Not bothering to grill Coltrane, Taylor says, "Goodbye. And Cheney, will you make sure nothing else changes, please? You guys have fun."

"Bye," Cheney and Coltrane say in unison.

Standing behind the desk as he ends the call, "Will you e-mail Taylor the proposal we prepared? And thank you for helping today. I'm sure I'll need it."

"No problem, Mr. Coltrane." And Cheney is off to her desk to e-mail Taylor.

A burst of energy came upon Taylor after her call with Coltrane. She is both zealous and raved at the new developments at the Center. If she receives 20 donated computers for the Center, she will hire a retired educator to tutor the youth in math and science. They can figure out how to use the computers—gadgets equaled excitement for them. Besides, they have a few iPads they share; Mac's functionality won't be foreign.

Taylor spends the next 40 minutes with a video yoga instructor who guides her through Downward Facing Dogs, Triangle poses, Warrior 1s, and Seated Forward Bends. Not only does this stretch her muscles, but it also relaxes her before she works. Just as the instructor says Namaste and before Taylor gets up off the hotel room floor, her phone vibrates against the small table. She doesn't recognize the number; only it's a LA number. She stretches toward the table without getting up to get her phone. "Hello."

Smiling through the receiver at the sound of her voice, "Hey beautiful," the husky voice of Isaiah Myers greets her. Without giving her a chance to respond, he continues in his naturally charming manner, "Did you get to rest?" He is genuinely concerned about the long hours she works.

"Hello, Mr. Myers. Yes, I did." Taylor radiates as she greets the handsome gent on the other end of the line. The same girlish feeling she had on her first crush in 7th-grade returns. What is it about this man that causes her to feel this way? Isaiah disturbs her thoughts. "Good. You up for a visitor?"

Playfully toying with him, "Who? I don't know anyone here."

"Hmmm, let's see whom you know in this city," he plays along.

"Could it be you are the visitor?" Taylor relishes this frolicsome chat with Isaiah.

"That is the right answer, dear," Isaiah enjoys the play-fulness as much as Taylor.

She recalls his plan, "Are you revising your suggested agenda?"

He is determined for her not to tell him No. Isaiah wants to spend time with Taylor. He is intrigued by her and recalls her beauty from the first time he saw her standing on the balcony at the Mayor's ball in Atlanta. She has an infectious smile; it does something to him every time she paints it on her gorgeous face. "If that's what it takes. Do you want to revise my proposed agenda?"

Taylor is in full relaxation mode after the yoga session. "I don't feel like getting out of my sweats. How about in-suite massages, room service, and your movie?" She realizes she invited this gorgeous specimen to an in-suite massage, but it is too late—the words slid off her tongue without think-ing. "I also have to review a proposal for the Foundation."

Surprised at her revisions and pleased he didn't hear the word No, "I don't want to suspend your work, but I also know you don't eat properly..."

Before he finishes, Taylor interjects, shifting to her playful mode, "And you want to become my chef?"

"No, but I want to ensure you get proper nourishment. And as I promised, I will do that whether you enjoy the meal with your geeky colleague or me."

They laugh at Isaiah's description of Hansen. "It's rare to see geeks in suits, but impressive the way he coordinates his suits with star wars t-shirts. You must admit his different color glasses, which rest on the tip of his nose; to match his t-shirts are humorous."

"Stop it; he's not a geek. He just has a whimsical sense of humor." Taylor and Hansen work well together. He is cool, smart, and doesn't care much about social derision. She enjoys their blossoming friendship. Bringing the conversation back to today's agenda, Taylor inquires. "Mr. Myers, what do you say to my revisions to your agenda?"

Isaiah can't see her body language but senses from her girlish ways Taylor wants to spend time with him, as much as he wants to with her. He hears the smile in her tone, causing him to grin. "Whatever pleases you, except I prefer not to have room service. I'll bring the grub, a bottle of wine, and the movie." He gives her a moment of consideration. In that instance, he ponders calling her on FaceTime, so he sees her expressions as they exchange banters. She doesn't object, he continues. "If you want dessert, we can order dessert from room service. I need a couple of hours. See you at about 5:30 p.m.?"

Isaiah is ecstatic with Taylor's adjustments to their plan. He decided he would love her the first night he laid eyes on her. And she's opening the possibility by letting him get to know her. He would eventually lay it all on the line because he doesn't want to wonder "what if." But he risks the disappointment of losing her. Chills line his spine.

Taylor imagines receiving the love she hears in Isaiah's voice, but quickly flees from her thought. "5:30 p.m. is a perfect time. I'll schedule the massages for 6:00 p.m. Oh, Mr. Myers, may I ask a favor?"

"Sure; Whatcha got?" Isaiah is startled by her request. She never asks for anything.

"Will you bring dark chocolate-covered almonds for me, please?" Isaiah hears Taylor's apprehension and wonders why she is guarded.

"Interesting request... I'll see what I can do. See you in a few hours." Isaiah never purchased dark chocolate-covered almonds. He doesn't know where to buy them. She was specific in her request, eliminating purchasing a bag of almonds from the gas station.

"Ciao!" Taylor presses end and retreats to the bedroom for her computer. Maybe she should donate her computer to the Foundation and use a dinosaur (as Coltrane referred to them). She'd ask Dulaney to contribute one, and she'd fill the shortfall. There are 20 active youth at the Center. She would reach out to firms she's worked with and pin the Mayor and the DA for donations. Coltrane is right—why hasn't she done this?

Opening the mail app on her computer, Taylor downloads the attachment to Cheney's e-mail. Impressed with the proposal, she makes minor revisions and e-mails it back to Cheney with her approval. She went to the business center and printed three copies, signed, and overnighted to Coltrane in case he faced issues with her electronic signature. Making slight modification to clauses in the original proposal that do not apply to law firms, she distributed it to select firms. She'd hand-deliver a request to Mr. Daniels on Monday. When Taylor finishes circulating proposals, she presses the speed dial for Dulaney.

Dulaney picks up on half a ring. She is excited to hear about the clothing the stylist selected for Taylor. And she hasn't talked to her best friend in weeks. "Hey, Tay! How are you? How's the trial? I'm sorry I didn't send your clothes. Did you like the stylist?" On the one hand, Taylor is shocked Dulaney is so joyful; but she is delighted to hear the happiness in Dulaney's voice. She misses her.

Just as triumphant, Taylor greets Dulaney. "Girl, I am the lawyer. But you have mad interrogation skills." They need not speak words to say they miss each other. "How are you? Why haven't you responded to my calls/texts?" It was selfish of Dulaney not to let her know she is well. She called her every day since she arrived in Los Angeles; Dulaney never answered, nor did she call back.

Dulaney hears concern in Taylor's voice. She knows it was unkind not to let Taylor know she's well. She let her stubbornness get the best of her. "I'm good. I feel great! Are you mad about the stylist? Did she make good selections?" Taylor is reminded she did not see clothes when she returned to the hotel last evening. The stylist said she'd deliver the clothes and shoes to her at the hotel.

"D, hold on a second," Taylor calls the front desk from the hotel phone to check for her delivery.

"Ms. Alexander, yes, ma'am. There is a delivery for you. I'll send it right up," the lady who answered the phone is apologetic.

Hanging up the hotel phone and returning to hers, Taylor explains to Dulaney. "D, the stylist came by the office yesterday to take measurements. She delivered the clothes, but not to my suite." Taylor walks the few steps from the small sofa to the suite door in anticipation of a knock. "The concierge is sending them up. I'm sure based on your strict instructions; she did well." Taylor teases Dulaney. She recalls the stylist reading from what appeared to be cue cards. Her tone changes to seriousness, but not scolding. "How are you, D?"

Dulaney primed for this conversation a million times over. But no amount of preparation serves her now. She knows Taylor won't agree with her decision, but she is committed to seeing it through. Dulaney starts slowly. "I have news"—with a rapid finish—"but don't come through the phone."

"D, what's going on?" Taylor's curiosity develops into unease.

Dulaney is eager, but she hopes fear doesn't overcome Taylor. She blurts out, "I am going back on stage." There is absolute silence on the line. After what seems like forever, Dulaney chimes in. "It's been so long since I was in the studio and more than a year since I was on stage." The appeal in Dulaney's voice is unmistakable. Taylor opens her mouth to speak but, no words come out; she is completely and utterly traumatized.

"Tay, are you there?" Dulaney appreciates Taylor's trepidation. She was her rock for the past year. Taylor fed her, bathed her, and held her hair as she puked. She never left her side. But Dulaney's mind is made. She hopes Taylor understands she needs to feel the stage again, even if it's her last time.

"Are you up to it?" Her words are straightaway as she processes Dulaney's news. Taylor doesn't want to discourage. She hears the cry in Dulaney's voice. But she fears Dulaney isn't physically ready to perform.

Dulaney reiterates her decision with compassion for Taylor's anxiety. "Taylor, I want to do this. I know you are scared for me; so am I. But I need to do this."

The sob in Dulaney's voice overwhelms Taylor. So she supports her best friend while also weighing other factors. She speaks with a pureness Dulaney easily recognizes. "I know you want to, but can you?" Taylor frees a stifled sigh.

Dulaney pleads her case, sounding like a preacher's kid. "I can do all things through Christ who strengthens me. Isn't that what His word says in Philippians 4:13? Don't we stand on His word in all circumstances? Why is this one different, Tay?" Dulaney pauses but not long enough for a reply from Taylor before she continues. "Taylor, when you left for LA, I realized it is time I stop letting this thing dictate my life. God has been first my entire life, and I will let nothing change that now. My God moves mountains and parts seas, heals the sick, and raises the dead. It's time I speak to my mountain." Without taking a breath, Dulaney describes her awestruck moment. "I sat in the park yesterday meditating in the alcove by the water. I watched the water sway and imagined God telling Moses to lift his staff and stretch his hand over the sea to stop the Red Sea flow so the children of Israel could get to the other side. I can't do the writer of Exodus justice, but can you envision that, Tay? Can you envision the water swaying back and forth, standing as walls on each side of you? Do you know the depth of the sea? Ever wonder what would have happened had Moses' faith crumbled? God is the same today as He was then. If He parted the Red Sea to create a dry path for the children of Israel to cross to the other side and then with the same instruction to Moses join the sea back together and engulf Pharaoh and his entire army with the same water that protected the people of Israel, why do you think God will not give me what I need to get on stage and do what I love."

Everything in her wants to debate Dulaney. But she has nothing. Dulaney is right. God is omniscient. "When is your show?"

"I know that's difficult for you. It's at the Staples Center in a few weeks." Dulaney is out of breath from the sermon she just preached to Taylor.

"I will be there front row and center." Taylor digs deep for strength. She wants to hug her best friend with reassurance of support. In her mind, she is coordinating medics and a nurse practitioner with IV fluids backstage, just in case. However, she does not share her thoughts with Dulaney. For as long as Dulaney's performed, she has never missed her concerts. She won't start now.

Dulaney changes topics, shifting the energy of their conversation. "Great! Did the clothes arrive?" She is eager to hear Taylor's reaction to the pieces the stylist selected.

Taylor stands in the tiny foyer where the mirror is on the wall, sliding her feet into the sexiest, strappy, navy blue sandal. She turns her feet on the edge of her toe to get a good look at the heel and then back flat to get a full side view. "I usually like to keep it classic in the courtroom, but I'll have to sashay in this shoe." Taylor admires the stiletto, capturing a photo which she texts to Dulaney.

Thrilled that Taylor likes the stiletto, Dulaney nudges her to the matching clothing. "Niiiiicccccceeeee! It pairs with the classic navy double-breasted dress." Dulaney gave the stylist specifics on the pieces Taylor likes. Something about the right shoe boosts Taylor's confidence, and she wants her to be at her best in the courtroom.

"How do you know?" Taylor fastens the buttons on the dress Dulaney described as she adorns the way it snugs her hip. She turns in the mirror—this foyer is too small for a fashion runway. "Where did you find this lady? And how much did this set you back because I am not paying you back? You were supposed to ship my clothes, not hire a stylist."

Dulaney giggles. She badgered Taylor throughout school to become a lawyer. Taylor always asks questions, and she doesn't mind a fair debate. "Can't I do something nice for my best friend?"

"As long as your best friend does not have to write you a check in return; yes, you may."

"Then consider it my act of kindness for one who always gives selflessly." Taylor has her ways, but one thing you cannot challenge is her gift of giving.

Dulaney's mention of giving triggers Taylor's memory. "Thank you, D. Speaking of giving, will you donate a computer to the Foundation? If it helps, I can send one pair of shoes back as a plea bargain."

This girl does not know how to shut off her legal mind, not even for a minute. "I am not that frugal! You don't have to bargain. I am happy to buy your rugrats a computer."

Recalling Coltrane's reference to her kids as knuckleheads, Taylor squeals into the phone, "Why y'all always picking on my kids? And you know you are cheap."

"I am responsible, not cheap. There is a difference, my friend." Dulaney is a minimalist and does not spend spontaneously.

"Are you suggesting I am irresponsible?"

"Not in the least, but if the shoe fits..."

Taylor cuts Dulaney off as she clasped the shoe and turns in the mirror. "This shoe fits perfectly. And the dress is classic—love it!"

As Taylor moves to the chair where the garment bag lays, she notices a pants suit. Her first thought is Dulaney knows I don't wear pants in the courtroom. Surprisingly, she is impressed when she removes it from the bag. Continuing to share details of the garments with Dulaney, "I might break my rule with this one." She admires the pants suit through the mirror in the much-too-small-foyer.

"You like the pants suit; don't you? I hesitated, but it suits you—no pun intended."

"I do. Where did you find the stylist?"

"I am happy you appreciate the wardrobe. Several years ago, Coltrane hired her to dress me for an event. I never discarded her card."

"Speaking of Coltrane. Have you talked with him?"

"No. And can we end this line of questioning, please?" There are things about her and Coltrane's relationship to which Taylor is not privy. Dulaney is not now ready, nor does she think she will ever be prepared to discuss.

"Yup! Thank you for the outfits. I love them." Taylor respects Dulaney's wish. She will eventually come face-to-face with her issues with Coltrane. But Taylor will not bark up that tree today. The firmness in Dulaney's voice says it all. Keeping the conversation pleasant, "Maybe you can stay a few days on the front or back end of your trip. We can visit Napa or Sonoma."

They always talked about visiting the vineyards. Since they will be in the region, it is an excellent idea. "Let's do it! I'll let you know my schedule once it's confirmed."

Schedule, wait, what? Dulaney only mentioned a show at Staples Center. "What do you mean schedule? I thought you are doing one show." Taylor's concern rose again.

Dulaney committed to three shows, starting in Atlanta, then to New York, and ending in Los Angeles. She will spoon-feed the information to Taylor; otherwise, she over-reacts. "I'll text you the details. Plan the trip to the vineyard, and we'll catch up later." Dulaney ends the call before she and Taylor revisits her decision to perform.

Taylor held the phone a few seconds after Dulaney hung up, wondering if there is more to this show. She tosses the phone on the sofa and continues fitting the clothes. Each piece persuades her Dulaney either selected them or provided undeniable details—there is no way the stylist knows her taste to this degree. Each ensemble speaks to a different side of her in the courtroom. Without guidance, the stylist wouldn't know those details.

She loves the apparel. Her favorite is the navy double-breasted dress. She hung the clothes in the closet, placing her shoes neatly on the shelf. She has two hours to review case material. And she must schedule the massages. She didn't think about it when she suggested it, but she isn't sure an in-room massage with a man she's known for a short while is a great idea. Should they have gone to the spa? "Dear Lord, please pour out an overflowing of your anointing in this suite," Taylor whispers out loud.

She spreads the material from the file over the small table. She needs to make sure every 'I' is dotted and every 'T' crossed. Further, she must anticipate the prosecution's curveballs. Taylor becomes consumed in the material and loses track of time until she hears a light tap on the suite's door. Suddenly, she remembers she absentmindedly forgot to schedule the massages. They say God watches out for babies and fools. And it is quite foolish of her to have in-room massages with this man. It isn't until she opens the door and Isaiah stands smelling and looking good that she realizes she didn't bother checking her appearance. He dressed casually in jeans and a button-down with the collar open. She sees his arm muscles penetrating through the cotton. The jeans paste onto his hamstrings, quads, and buttocks oh so perfectly. And the loafers—which he wears sockless—are well shined. "Hi! Come in."

Isaiah enters the suite. Whatever food is in the bag smells as good as him. "Where should I place these?" he asks, raising each arm calling attention to the bags.

Taylor is red with embarrassment. Her hair is in a messy bun. She has no lip-gloss on. Her sweats and tee are not neatly groomed. She's suddenly curious what he thinks of her look. "Oh! Sorry about that. Put them here on the counter." Taylor points to the empty counter. "Forgive me for looking like a bum. I lost track of time."

Isaiah didn't mind if she wore coveralls drenched in oil. She is modestly beautiful. "Work has its way of dominating the best of us. You look great. I like the sweats." Isaiah soothes while he surveys her sculpted arms and her quads peeking through the material of her sweats. "You hungry now? Do you need to finish?" He examines the room and her because she doesn't appear to be ready for company.

Looking back and forth between the papers scattered on the table and Isaiah—it is clear she needs more time—"Do you mind giving me a few minutes to wrap up? I won't be long."

A warm smile plasters his face as he looks into her brown eyes, batting through the red spectacles he's sure she doesn't recall are on her face. "Sure; do your thing. Is there a docking station in the suite?" Isaiah would accommodate the five-foot-six caramel-colored beauty by combing through emails and listening to classical music. He explores the area awaiting Taylor's response.

"The docking station is in the bedroom. I am not sure if it's removable, but you can check." Taylor kicks herself for inviting him to the bedroom. She didn't dress the bed and kindly excused housekeeping. Isaiah circles and then points toward the bedroom, "In here?"

"Yup; in there."

He returns with the docking station in tow, and soon after that, Taylor hears the sounds of Johann Sebastian Bach—Air in D minor from the 3rd orchestral suite. She loves classical music and is pleasantly surprised to listen to it coming from his playlist. "Is this okay," Isaiah imposes on Taylor's thoughts. "If you don't like classical, I can tune it to jazz or R&B."

"Bach suites me just fine." Taylor peeks at him from over the red reading glasses. Isaiah is equally impressed; she recognizes the tune. Taylor's head goes back to her material, and Isaiah responds to e-mail on his tablet. He threw his carrier in his car just in case the beauty seated before him obsessed over work. After an unknown amount of time elapsed, when his growling stomach reminds Isaiah it's time to eat, he eases to the table where Taylor's head is buried in papers.

"Counselor, should I feed you intravenously?" Taylor looks up and realizes more than just a few minutes passed. It's easy for work to occupy her. "I'm so sorry. Why didn't you say something?"

Isaiah stands over her with his charm emanating—his silky brown skin complimented the dimples, and his grin is intoxicating. The energy between them lit the air like a force of lightning as they cast each other wanton looks. In an effortlessly seductive tone, "I am saying something now. Is this a good time to break?" He peers at her rapturously.

"Yes, give me 5 minutes." This man affects her profoundly. And she believes he knows it.

Realizing his stare made her uncomfortable, he lifted his gaze. "I'll warm the food if you don't mind me in your kitchen." Isaiah points to the area deemed the kitchen. They smile, and he steps into that area. He fumbles around for glasses, finally finding one Taylor used to drink wine and another in a small hanging space. He cleans the glasses, pours a sip of wine to sample in one, and makes the same three steps back to Taylor, handing her the glass. After she swirls, smells, and sips, he fills her raised glass and his when he is back at the counter. After heating the veggies and getting Taylor's choice of chicken, fish, or steak, they are all set for dinner—which they eat on the sofa—Taylor's file is scattered on the table. "So what's with the dark chocolate-covered almonds?"

Isaiah's question reminds Taylor of her request. "Did you bring them?" Taylor asks inquisitively and gives him a side-glance.

"Yes, but given the labor required, I must know if they are a fave?" Isaiah exaggerated.

"They are a favorite, but more importantly, they complement the wine."

Isaiah glares at Taylor as they sipped from their glasses. He engages her in conversation by calling to her attention they enjoy wine and food pairing; they are workaholics—the last several hours prove that hypothesis. His tone becomes jovial as he continues, "So I ask Counselor, would you please not jump off the ledge? I would love to get to know you better."

Laughing lightly, "I do not intend to jump—not that night nor ever. I like me."

"I like you too." Isaiah stuns Taylor. She fumbles with the wineglass, almost wasting wine in her lap.

Quickly regaining composure and almost as if she's cross-examining a witness, "How do you know that, Mr. Myers?" Taylor sits back, so she has a direct line of sight to Isaiah's face. His features are captivating—thick natural eyebrows, sumptuous full lips, and high, sculpted cheekbones.

With unparalleled confidence and no reluctance, "Kindred spirits, Counselor." Isaiah grins. Taylor is taken aback.

"So tell me, Mr. Myers, what's your story?" Taylor comes out of the trance Isaiah's response cast her into and back to earth.

"Whatever do you mean?" Isaiah asks with an unfounded genuineness.

True to form, as if she has a witness on the stand, "Tell me what you think I don't want to know—or shouldn't—about Isaiah Myers." Taylor places her glass on the floor, sits back, and focuses.

With the utmost confidence and complete control, "Why don't I start with the basics? Isaiah Monroe Myers. Single. One daughter—Nyla—8 years old, will go to the end of the world and back for her. Her mother is Lauren Jets. We share custody, two weeks each a month, splitting holidays. Adjusting schedules is commonplace, but we never infringe on the other's time. I own Myers & Associates, where we educate young stars in finance and investments. Biochemical engineering was my previous profession. I work out daily in the gym in my office building, where I also own a condo. You know one hobby—wine tasting and pairing; the other is a little dangerous if proper precautions aren't taken."

Taylor gives him a weird look but does not interrupt.

"I enjoy shooting at the local range, but I have years of training, and I am never unsupervised. You know my brother and my uncle. And I think that does it for the basics."

His summary is in line with what Detective Cathy provided. She catalogs the shooting hobby, though she doesn't probe. Hansen questioned it when Cathy gave her readout of him. He wouldn't, would he? She buries the thought as she did when Hansen mentioned it. They spent the rest of the evening engrossed in conversation, listening to classical music—from Bach to Chopin to Mozart and Beethoven. He is a delight, and she likes spending time with him. "It is well beyond my bedtime, and you need your rest. I better get going."

"Geesh, is it 1:40 a.m.?" Taylor could not believe the time passed.

"Yes, sunshine. As much as I enjoy your company, I better get going." Isaiah knows he is treading on dangerous territory because while his mind tells him he needs to leave, all he wants to do is take Taylor in his arms and kiss her.

Taylor recognizes his uneasiness. "Okay. Well, be careful." She contemplates hugging him. They stand in awkward silence, fixated. Isaiah reaches for her hand, instinctively stroking her soft palm. She shivers, causing his arousal. But she isn't cold. His eyes dart to the up-and-down motion of her breast as she respires intensely. The thin material of her tee does nothing to protect her from the warmth of his body. Taylor doesn't know how or when, but she is off her feet into Isaiah's arms. His lips captivate hers, and his tongue explores the angles of her mouth. She wants to resist—at least that's what she thought—but his mouth is warm against hers. She feels protected in his arms (although she doesn't know what she needs protecting from). Her repressed stress frees itself as he pulls her into his embrace. He tightens his squeeze, and she relaxes in his arms, comforted. That frisson turns her on. Taylor no longer fights her desires. Gone is her nervousness, replaced by the fire Isaiah evokes in her.

The morning sun invites itself into the bedroom of Taylor's suite, as it does every morning. She slept peacefully but is alarmed, realizing she is in Isaiah's arms. He felt her body tense. Brushing her hair from the side of her face, "You okay, Counselor?"

Taylor wants to scream. She emptied her cookie jar. So no, she isn't okay. I mean, yes, technically, she is okay; but no, she isn't. She silently prays. God, please forgive. By this time, Isaiah is resting on one elbow. He feels the anxiety emitting from Taylor's body. Her energy is strong and powerful. He reaches for her hand, bows his head, and prays. "Father God, we cry to you this morning for forgiveness. While we strive to live in your perfect will, we fell short of your glory, consumed by the lust of our flesh. We ask first for forgiveness for Taylor and then for myself, for we sinned against you. We love you. We honor you. And we praise your holy and most precious name. In Jesus' name. Amen."

Taylor thought she fainted. No man—ever—prayed with or for her, except her dad. She doesn't even recall Mr. Hunt outwardly praying for her.

"Are you familiar with the book of Deuteronomy?" Isaiah brings Taylor back from wherever she was. She was in a spell; she can't explain it.

"Yes, chapter 30, right?"

"Yes, can't remember the exact verse. Counselor, we will never repeat this mistake—well, wait, not mistake because I loved—okay, I'm getting off track. What I'm trying to say is you are worth the wait, and I am willing to wait."

Taylor is sure she is insentient. Has he called the paramedics to resuscitate her because she is sure no oxygen is flowing through her body? She cannot move or speak. She lies numb. Isaiah shakes her, "Counselor?" a tinged of nervousness in his voice.

Taylor clears her throat as air once again flows, "Huh," is all Taylor gets out. Isaiah sits against the headboard and pulls Taylor into his arms. "You're making me nervous, Counselor. You are never quiet." She doesn't know if she is in shock or semi-consciousness. Isaiah holds her until she is again coherent.

He suggests they go for a run, sensing Taylor needs fresh air, and then grab brunch. Taylor doesn't object. The fresh air will do her good. After their hike on Runyon Canyon, they eat breakfast at one of those all-day breakfast places. The run was refreshing for Taylor and gave her back her brain. "Listen, Isaiah..."

Stunned, she greets him by name, "I believe that's the first time you said my first name," he intervenes.

Taylor smiles. "Mr. Myers..."

"Now that's my girl." Isaiah is relieved.

Not wanting their playful flirting to distract her, Taylor relaxes in her natural character. "Are you going to let me finish, Mr. Myers?"

"She's back," Isaiah teases.

"Yes, she is. I heard you this morning. I am not sure if I was unconscious or not, but..." Taylor fumbles for words. She became apprehensive, and the desire to escape overwhelmed her. "... Let's just say I heard you this morning. And thank you, thank you for praying for and with me."

Isaiah recognizes the change in her demeanor. He is curious because this is a side of her he hasn't seen. She is always in Counselor mode, but not now. She is bashful, maybe even timid. "What were you about to say?" Isaiah presses with caution.

"It doesn't matter." Taylor is becoming unglued and needs to get away. Her emotions heighten, but she wills herself to not show venerability, not in public.

Isaiah doesn't want to force her, but he wants to explore this angle. He pushes, but not forcefully. He needs her to see it is safe to be transparent with him. "It matters to me. I'll let it be for now if you promise to tell me later." Isaiah doesn't like her evasiveness, but he doesn't want to upset her.

"Let's head back. I've got a few things to do before morning." Taylor avoids looking at him.

Isaiah is more than alarmed at Taylor's change in behavior. So he insists, "Taylor, what is it?" Taylor does not respond. She stands, kisses Isaiah on the forehead, and says, "Thank you for your gentleness, for caring, for..." and she leaves the restaurant, running hard and as fast as she can back to the hotel. How is she to tell this man she lost her virginity to him? It is apparent he doesn't realize it. Is she falling in love with a man she's known for eight weeks? Is that even possible? Besides, she will return to Atlanta after the trial. Speaking of the trial, that's her focus. It is the reason she's in Los Angeles.

When she reaches her suite, housekeeping had cleaned—thank God she isn't reminded of her act. She enjoyed the intimacy she shared with Isaiah. She loves what she knows about him. But she can't focus on him. She has a man—Isaiah's brother—to keep out of jail; that's her concentration. Taylor spent the rest of the day meditating, praying, and preparing for trial. After a long and hot soak in the whirlpool tub, she is ready to retire under the soft sheets. Before she turns the light out, she texts *Goodnight* to Isaiah. He doesn't respond.

Before Isaiah turned in for the evening, he left a message on Taylor's voice mail as he did many times before. He is convinced she has not listened to them because he left a crazy one on purpose, and she never mentioned it.

CHAPTER 4

The Goodnight Text

Preparing for his morning run, Isaiah connects his headphones to his cell. He notices Taylor sent a text last night that reads *Goodnight.* His chest thumps rapidly. How did I miss her text? They didn't talk since she abruptly ran out of the restaurant during brunch yesterday. He thinks about the weight of his non-responsiveness and it excogitates his worry. Will it further influence her mood?

The morning air is fresh with no visible smog. After an exhilarating run, Isaiah stops in his building's gym for strength training. Beads of sweat slide slowly down his biceps and trace his cut muscles before dripping to the floor. Working out releases stress from his body, and this morning he needs it. He can't stop thinking about the sudden shift in Taylor's attitude. They enjoyed a lovely evening and an incredible workout the next morning—at least in his mind. Obviously, her recollection is altered. What happened? Did he miss something?

He invites Boyd, who is much more in tune with the ladies, to breakfast to make sense of it. Boyd's ladies refer to him as the current-day Samson—for his strength and sex appeal. It's not unusual for him to wake up to a hot feminine body with a pair of curvaceous buttocks cuddled alongside him. He is suave, smooth, and not only knows what the ladies want, but he also gives it to them. Boyd aims to please. He tauntingly torments his ladies by appealing to their senses.

Boyd arrives at the café before Isaiah. He wonders why Isaiah invited him for breakfast; they rarely dine together. He sees a cookbook with an erotic name in the display of products and fantasizes about exploring every inch of her stretched across his kitchen counter while she reads a recipe to him. His thoughts are insanely ravenous, which his dear brother disturbs as he sits opposite him at the table. "What scandalous lane is your imagination traveling?"

"What's up, man? Or shall I say who has your panties in a knot?" Boyd presumes Taylor, his attorney, is the reason Isaiah seeks advice from his younger brother. He and Isaiah jab at each other until the waiter approaches, "Ready to order?" They place orders and resume their brotherly bantering.

"Man, must you always eat healthily?" Boyd's expression as he pesters Isaiah about his eating habits resembles a five-year-old mocking his mother.

"Seriously, who eats scrambled tofu? Can't you get some damn scrambled eggs like the rest of us?" Boyd's badgering continues. He reads from the menu, "spinach, spicy cashew aioli, and pickled carrots..." Isaiah agitates his brother, who is bothered by his food choices with sarcasm. "Maybe you should try a healthy dish or two. I'm happy to share."

Boyd flings the menu at Isaiah, changing the conversation. "What's going on, man?" Isaiah catches the menu mid-air and places it on the table. He sits back in his chair before answering his brother. "Man, how in the world do you survive multiple ladies? I can't decode one." Boyd's laughter rebounds off the walls of the restaurant.

"Is it my sexy attorney you cannot crack?" The scowl on Isaiah's face warns Boyd he better not cross the line.

"Dude, you're whipped?" Boyd shakes his head dramatically—all the while smirking, "You always fall for the prim & proper ones."

Isaiah sulks at Boyd's theatrics. The palms of his hands meet his forehead, and he drops his elbows onto the table. Confounded, he shares his dilemma. "We spent a lovely evening together—we both worked..."

"You worked on a date. Problem 1. Let's hear the rest." Boyd is beside himself. Who works on a date?

"She worked on your case, fool!"

"That's the only exception. Go on."

Isaiah tosses the paper napkin at Boyd before he resumes. "Like I said, we worked a bit, ate dinner, and listened to music as we sip wine over great conversation. We went for a hike in Runyon Park after we woke the next morning and grabbed brunch afterward."

"Wait! Did you say after we woke—as in she spent the night?" Boyd leans in attentively and observes Isaiah's temperament.

"Will you keep interrupting me? Or let me tell you what happened?"

"Finish, man. But did she spend the night?"

Isaiah is careful because he does not want another dispersing of information (as Taylor so eloquently put it). He remembers sharing one of his and Taylor's conversations with Boyd. "I spent the night at her hotel suite." Isaiah watches Boyd closely, waiting for a reaction.

"Is there a couch in her hotel suite and is that where you slept?" Isaiah takes too long to answer.

"The struggle on your face says it all, man. This is why I don't fall in love. You look pitiful!"

"Are you here to help? Or take stabs at me?"

"Do you regret it?" Boyd asks.

"Man, it was angelic," Isaiah's voice trembles. If Boyd suggests to Taylor Isaiah shared their intimacy with him, she won't ever speak to him again. "Somewhere between waking and brunch, she does a 360. The assertive girl becomes timid—unsociable. She looks away from me instead of making eye contact with me. Hell, she hardly talked to me during brunch. Then, she gets up and runs like hell out of the restaurant." Isaiah looks hopelessly to his younger brother for relationship advice.

"Damn! That's cold."

"Boyd, please don't..." Before Isaiah finishes his appeal, Boyd assures him he has nothing to worry about.

"I'd never, bro. But you should take a page out of my book. Mutual satisfaction, no headaches." Boyd has sexual encounters all the time. But his emotions are off-limits. He plays the game, but he is transparent, letting everyone know he's not in it for emotional entanglement.

"Let me ask. Don't think I am prying for the sake of prying." Boyd asks about the events of Isaiah's recent date with Taylor. Isaiah's answers help formulate a logical reason for Taylor's precipitous, uncharacteristic behavior. Boyd invests time studying ladies. In college, he set out to prove a hypothesis about his then-girlfriend. It fueled his desire to understand why girls do what they do, behave when, why, and how they do. He unearthed valuable traits about the female, and it's afforded him an advantage with the ladies. When he finishes inquiring, he sensitively suggests, "Man, sounds like you are her first. WTF. That's a big deal!"

"Dude, that's crazy! She's a grown-ass woman." Boyd's advice jolts Isaiah. Taylor is strong, independent, and fierce; indeed, she dated before him. Boyd can't be right about this. Does she ascribe to her value based on sexual purity? "Wouldn't I have sensed it?" Isaiah asks, not bidding an answer. "Isn't there a code that says a girl must tell you if she's a virgin?"

"Don't freak out. But being her first comes with a responsibility that some men don't want to shoulder. But you want the relationship, the intimacy. She likes you. She is scared because she doesn't know how to tell you. Cut her some slack."

The brothers finish their breakfast—Isaiah hardly touches his food. Boyd taunts him about the scrambled tofu and offers to take him to get real scrambled eggs, toast, and bacon—an American breakfast. Isaiah pays the waiter, not realizing Boyd included the cookbook. Boyd sarcastically thanks him for the cookbook, and they part in opposite directions from the restaurant.

Isaiah sits in his car in absolute awe, reliving his conversation with Boyd. He butt dials Taylor. Thank God she does not answer. He collects his thoughts as he stares onto Sante Fe Avenue. The hotel is roughly three miles from the restaurant. He considers going by there, but Taylor called him a stalker once, so it's probably not a good idea. Instead, he turns the convertible around and heads away from downtown and out of the Arts District.

Isaiah bows to his assistant, who is on the phone when he walks past her desk to his office. He has about an hour before his client's press conference. Taking a seat behind his desk, he spins his chair and views the hustle and bustle of the busy streets. He can't get Taylor off his mind. Was she pure?

A knock on the door sometime later intrudes on his thoughts. His assistant reminds him of the press conference and informs him his client is in the waiting area. Isaiah can't believe he got lost in his reflections. He didn't get any work done in the past hour because thoughts of Taylor played endlessly on his mind. The smell of her perfume is in the air, even when she isn't around. He imagined her hands moving up his thighs, her lips tenderly touching his. His mind burns with illusions, incapable of satisfying him. He has an insatiable hunger for her. He remembers Taylor in Counselor mode, where she is polished and confident, assertive but graceful. She is beautiful, driven, and smart, and Isaiah finds himself falling for every part of her. He envisioned her with her hair loosely dangling curls below her shoulders. In her sweats and tank, he recalls her small waist and the delicate curves of her hips. As sensual as she is suited up, she is mesmeric in her sweats—an absolute turn-on.

Isaiah pauses at his assistant's desk on his way to greet his client, "Joi, do you mind making dinner reservations for two at LA Prime for 7:30 p.m.?" He commences to the waiting room to greet his client and then head to the press conference. Isaiah doesn't know if Taylor will have dinner with him, but he wants to be prepared. He never responded to her Goodnight text, but he hopes it doesn't adversely affect her mood. He texts her—*Hey Beautiful, have dinner with me tonight. 7:30? LA Prime?* The restaurant isn't far from either her office or hotel. She's usually at the office until seven-ish. Now off to the press conference he goes.

The press conference was a shit show between his client's bad attitude and the media. His client is undoubtedly one of the most talented in the league—gifted beyond grace—but this kid has an ego the size of North America. And he wears the chip on his shoulder loudly. No amount of subterfuge can disguise the owner's desire to trade him.

When Isaiah returns to his office, he realizes Taylor didn't respond to his text. He thought little of it at first; after all, she is a working woman. But as time crept into the late afternoon and she still had not responded, he picked up the phone and called her. Cathy answers in her pleasant, polite tone, and after his usual small talk, she transfers him to Taylor's line. He hopes the Counselor answers, but no such luck.

Taylor is seated behind the mahogany desk when the red light flickers on the desk phone. She guesses it was Isaiah and is reminded of his text earlier, inviting her to dinner. She doesn't want to avoid him. By nature, she isn't mean-spirited, but she also isn't ready to see him. She responds to his invitation—thank you, but I have a lot of work to do. Rain check? That isn't so bad, is it? While she said no to tonight, she indicated her desire to have dinner on another occasion. Both that night and him are always on her mind. While she has morals and values, she didn't set out to save herself until she married. The notion her first time would be special didn't escape her. She didn't necessarily have to be in a committed relationship, but at least with someone who cares about her on some level, someone to consider her pleasure as much as his own. Until Isaiah, no one measured up. A call to Dulaney is apropos.

She could no longer concentrate, so Taylor left the office early. A run and fresh air may clear her head. The hike on Runyon Park is an invigorating workout. Both times she hiked Runyon Canyon Road, which is the least challenging trail. When she went with Isaiah, they took the route in reverse; climbing the steps and the slopes (both are pretty steep) stimulates the muscles. The downtown views are stunning. Today she wants a test, the challenging route of Hero's Trail. She's told this route yields superlative views to the south and west.

Before she leaves, Taylor stops by Mr. Daniels' office. The glass wall reveals he is not on the phone, so she taps lightly and peeks in. "Got a minute?" Standing in front of his European desk, Taylor hands Mr. Daniels the request to donate a computer for the Foundation. "Will you ensure the Managing Partner gets this, please?" Accepting the brown manila envelope but unsure of its contents, Mr. Daniels responds, "Coming on board full time?"

Self-consciously shaking her head, Taylor is decisive in her response, "No sir, not at all! It's a request for a donation for my youth center." Mr. Daniels smiles admirably and opens the envelope, "Young lady, we need more of you. You're doing good in the world, and you have our support." He presses a button on his desk phone and speaks, "Will you purchase ten computers as a donation? Ms. Alexander will provide the delivery instructions."

Did she hear him correctly? Taylor stands in astonishment. She asked for one computer. Mr. Daniels gives Taylor the same envelope she placed in his hand and spouts out instructions. "Stop by Finance. They need delivery information." Taylor is in disbelief, but she thanks Mr. Daniels. "The kids will be delighted, and I am grateful. Thank you." As she reaches the doorway, "I'm leaving earlier than usual today. If anything comes up, Cathy knows how to reach me." Mr. Daniels nods, and Taylor goes down the corridor to Finance.

After she provides the details to the pleasant young lady in the Finance department, Taylor returns to her office, gathers her things, and proceeds to the conference room where Hansen's face is buried in a file folder. Cathy stands in the doorway, receiving instruction from him. Both are surprised when Taylor announces her departure for the day. Hansen clowns with her while Cathy express genuine concern. "Ms. Alexander, is everything okay." Cathy can't recall a day when Taylor left the office at 4:00 p.m. "Yes, Cathy. Thank you for asking." Taylor adjusts her portfolio on her shoulder, grips the folders she carries, and proceeds to the elevator.

Taylor second-guesses a hike on her way to the hotel because the air is polluted. When she arrives at her suite, she quickly changes into workout gear before changing her mind. It is muggy trekking up Hero's Trail. She stops briefly to hydrate and takes in her surroundings—the view is striking. She isn't to the top, but the view inspires her to keep moving up the trail. When she reaches the top, she has a real-time 360-degree panoramic view—clear blue sky with puffy white clouds, hills, greenery, and tall buildings in the background—she takes it all in. Taylor rests, placing her air pods in her ears to mediate as she savors the view.

After reflecting on the majestic scenery at the top of Runyon Canyon, Taylor makes her way back to her hotel, forcing all qualms of giving herself to Isaiah from her mind. She didn't consider her virginity unthinkable. She simply chose not to have random sex. In fact, research reveals many students graduate college without ever having sex. Why does society stigmatize both ends of the spectrum—either a girl is a slut or a virgin. She would call Dulaney for girl talk after she enjoys a calming champagne bath.

Eager to hear from her friend, "Hey, Tay! What's up?" Dulaney came through the stereo of Taylor's air pods. Taylor hears the background noise indicating Dulaney is in the studio. "Do you need to call me back?" Taylor's hope that Dulaney can talk shrank.

Excited at the replay of the lyrics she just laid over an electrifying track, she exclaims, "No, no! Listen to this." Dulaney is charged and wants to share that excitement with her friend.

"It sounds nice." Taylor is usually zealous to hear Dulaney's music, but right now, she finds it hard to be as overjoyed as Dulaney.

She grimaces at not being able to talk with Dulaney. They grew up sharing many of the same life experiences that their childhoods melded into one. Taylor wants to share this experience and her struggle but kindly releases Dulaney from the call. "I'll catch up with you later. The track is dope!"

Dulaney does not recognize the distress in Taylor's voice. She gushes over how good the track sounds and tells her friend she'll call her later.

Taylor sits with this one alone—and maybe that's what she needs—time to process alone. She's not sure why she freaked out. From what she knows of Isaiah, he is kind, intelligent, and an upstanding gentleman. Admittedly, there is undeniable sexual chemistry between them. He is that man who makes you realize there is more to life by merely looking at him. He exudes unparalleled masculinity that draws out a woman's complacency. And he is humbled. Despite all, losing her virginity to him has her unsettled. She cannot pinpoint why.

Later that night, Taylor slithers under the soft sheets and drowns her thoughts of Isaiah with music. Rarely does she listen to hip-hop to go to sleep, but she wants nothing to thrust her into a fantasy. She daydreamed earlier in the evening where she imagined categorically corrupt thoughts, and the illusions she had of things Isaiah did to her are scandalously sinful. Despite being immoral and wicked, they seem shockingly satisfying. She contemplated texting Isaiah goodnight as she did the night before, but decided against it.

She glances at her phone for the time; it is 10:30 p.m. She wonders if Isaiah is awake but, again, decides not to reach out. Her thoughts drift to the night Isaiah was there, sitting in the corner chair on his iPad. She glanced at him several times, checking him out. She remembers how struck she was by him in jeans and a white button-down—he is a good-looking, handsome man. And that voice—he speaks in a deep, erogenous voice—causing pulsations in unnamed parts of her body. The way his jeans fit perfectly across his firm thighs makes her heart thump. Who knew the arrogant man she met on the balcony in Atlanta would become her ever-waking desire.

The alert of her phone invades Taylor's reminiscing. The text read, *you consumed my every thought today*. It's from Isaiah. Taylor responds, *have a good night*, and turns the lamp off and covers her head with the soft sheets.

Isaiah read Taylor's text and let out a flustered sigh. For the life of him, he doesn't know what caused the change in her. And damn it, he cannot get her out of his mind! She has a way of putting every one of his male hormones on full alert, even when she isn't around him—the mere thought of her affects him the same way. She possesses an irresistible sensuality. Her utter unawareness of the depth of her appeal ensorcelled him.

Isaiah turns in for the night, hoping sleep will suspend his thoughts of Taylor. Who knew that the lady he rescued on the balcony in Atlanta would become his ever-waking desire.

CHAPTER 5

The Trial Begins

"Good morning," Mr. Daniels and Mayor Sellect greet Taylor and Hansen, who are in the conference room. Taylor is surprised to see the Mayor in Los Angeles. "Good morning, gentlemen."

Addressing the Mayor, "It is great you're here to support Boyd. But you shouldn't be in the courtroom." Taylor examines the Mayor before continuing her explanation. "If your theory of revenge holds any weight, your presence isn't wise," Taylor questioned the Mayor's involvement and his lack of transparency when she learned Boyd is his nephew. The Mayor advocated Judge Crane framed Boyd for the attempted murder of Detective Franklin. He reasoned it was revenge against him. She did not build her defense on the Mayor's revenge theory. But if the judge has an old ax to grind, it isn't smart for him to be in the courtroom.

In agreement with Taylor, "This is why I hired you, young lady. I will not appear in Court unless you give the word. I'm here for my nephew." The loud sound of the file Hansen accidentally drops distracts the Mayor and Taylor.

"Boyd and Isaiah have made great strides to rebuild their brotherhood since their fallout. I commend Isaiah for side-lining his differences and backing Boyd." Taylor has no clue to the Mayor's reference of the brothers' incongruence. His look says don't ask.

Taylor's radar goes on high alert. Could the brothers' differences have something to do with this case? The Mayor didn't divulge details, but she is indisputably exploring a beef between the brothers.

"Thank you for understanding, Mr. Mayor," and Taylor left the conference room en route to Cathy's desk. Cathy's fact-finding skills are exemplary; she does not need an in-vestigator. "Cathy, will you dig up anything you can find on the Myers brothers, please?" Taylor spoke quietly as she leaned over the reception desk for discretion.

Cathy asks Taylor to wait a minute. Taylor stands patiently while Cathy handles the phone lines. When she finishes, she gets clarity from Taylor. "Boyd Myers, Ms. Alexander?"

"Both." Taylor leans over the desk to avoid anyone overhearing her conversation. "I suspect there was a rivalry between them. I'm sorry, that's all I know." She is confident Cathy will uncover the details.

"I'll let you know what I find." Cathy is on to the next call. Boyd and Isaiah walk into the reception area as Taylor leaves to return to the conference room. Isaiah is uncertain about Taylor's interaction with him. They haven't spoken since she abruptly ran out of the restaurant during brunch on Sunday. He doesn't know what to expect. "Good morn-ing, gentlemen. Follow me." She is in pure Counselor mode. Isaiah has a feeling she will be in lawyer form for the days ahead. They trail her to the conference room.

When they reach the room, Taylor announces Boyd's arrival. "Our client is here. Let's get this party started."

Hansen interprets. "Translation: Time to head to the courthouse."

The Mayor talks to his nephews off in a corner. Hansen and Taylor gather their things and give them privacy. Shortly thereafter, the mayor and his nephews join them in the reception area. Taylor says, "Let's get going," and exits the door en route to the elevator.

At 9:00 sharp, the bailiff gets everyone's attention. "All rise. The Honorable Randall Crane. The Court's now in session. People vs. Mr. Boyd Meyers. Attempted Murder. Section 187."

The trial begins with the state's direct examination of LAPD Detective Talia, laying the foundation for later expert testimony and establishing chain of custody. When the prosecution finishes on direct, the defense team cross-examines the detective. "Detective Talia, I'd like to call your attention to September 7th. Did you respond to a crime scene in the summit of the Santa Monica Mountains?"

"Yes, I did." Detective Talia is no stranger to the witness stand. She has testified in many trials, and her calm demeanor indicates such.

Positioning herself in front of the witness stand and squared with the jury, Taylor continues her questioning. "Do you mind telling us what you observed when you arrived at the scene?"

Not flinching, the detective answers. "Yellow police tape secured the area at the location of the summit, just away from the drivable portion of Mulholland Drive. There was a path of blood that ran from the restrooms to the trail."

Stepping closer to the witness stand with her hands interlocked and resting below her waist, "Was the victim at the scene when you arrived?"

Shaking her head no as she replies to Taylor, who is moving closer to the witness stand, "No, EMS transported him to the hospital." Detective Talia shifts on the witness stand.

Resting her left arm on the witness stand, Taylor probes. "What did you do after you arrived? What's your protocol?" She doesn't move but listens closely as the detective explains.

"I photographed the scene intact." Detective Talia keeps eye contact with Taylor. "I videoed the scene with my phone. Today's technology is convenient. After that, I searched for evidence, documenting anything I came across."

Taylor takes a few steps towards the jury box and gestures to the jury when she asks, "Do you mind telling the jury what you searched for?"

Detective Talia turns to the jury in reaction to Taylor's gesture before she answers. "Any evidence of the injury, the weapon, any clue to what happened." She looks to the prosecution's table and then to the jury. "Specifically, I looked for expended firearms, fragments from a bullet. Also looked for tire marks, shoe impressions, anything left by the suspect." The detective looks back to Taylor as she completes her explanation, awaiting the next question.

Taylor walks to the defense's table, opens a manila folder, and scans the contents before continuing her cross. "Did you recover a weapon from the crime scene?" She raises her head enough to glance toward the witness stand.

"We did not recover the weapon. We canvassed the entire area but did not find it." She knows the jury will react to not recovering a weapon and glances in their direction.

Walking back to the witness stand, Taylor places a small object on the ledge before the witness. "Detective, tell us about the blood path you observed." Not waiting for an answer, she cross-examines. "Will you show on the diagram using the laser pointer"—and she points at the object she placed on the ledge of the witness stand—"where you observed the blood?"

"Yes. The blood trail—well, it wasn't a complete trail—but the blood was by the area of the bench." The detective picks up the laser pointer and hovers the red dot on the area.

"Did you find fragments or shell casings in that area?" Taylor walks back to the defense's table and retrieves papers as the detective responds.

"No, I did not."

Taylor returns to the witness stand holding the papers she just retrieved. Spreading them on the ledge, she remains. "I believe these are in evidence as State's exhibits 15-20; do you recognize these?"

Detective Talia picks up the papers, looks at them, and replies, "Yes, they are the photographs of the crime scene."

"Thank you, Detective. I have no further questions." Returning to the defense's table, Taylor takes her seat, examining the jury as she does so.

Both legal teams went back and forth on direct and cross-examination of witnesses in the case. After weeks of testimony, the prosecution didn't provide clear evidence the defendant shot the victim and dumped his wounded body in the mountains. All the evidence presented is circumstantial. The evidence Taylor presented did not tie the defendant to the shooting; he had no motive. She made a note to herself to follow up with Cathy to see what she discovered about the brothers' rivalry. The Mayor's remark of their differences lingered in her mind. She hasn't talked with Isaiah outside of the proceedings. Despite the significant evidence pointing to Boyd Myer's innocence, the jury looks flat. But this is no time to lose faith in justice, so Taylor presses on. To establish the defendant's fingerprints were not on any evidence collected from the crime scene, she will cross-examine the fingerprint expert.

The prosecution conducts its direct examination of the LAPD's fingerprint examiner, who testifies to the legal opinion that every fingerprint is unique and a fingerprint examiner can conclusively opine a match if, in his expert opinion, enough points of comparison are present to declare a match. Taylor does not attack the reliability of science. It's customary for the judge to allow the examiner to give an opinion. She establishes the assumptions inherent in fingerprint examination. Despite debates on conclusive fingerprint matches being unscientific, such testimony is accepted and generally admissible.

The defense calls Dr. Omen, who, on direct examination, provided testimony about the victim's wound. Taylor explores whether the bullet wound matches a definitive bullet or gun cartridge. The detective earlier admitted to not finding the weapon. Hence, the defense's primary purpose is to demonstrate the prosecution's speculation. "Dr. Omen, will you describe for the jury the victim's wounds at the time of your initial exam?"

"Sure. Detective Franklin presented with a gunshot wound to the chest consistent with close-range shootings.

The bullet tore through the left lung but made a clean exit." The doctor takes his time and summarizes his examination of the victim's wound.

"Thank you." Taylor stands in front of the witness stand, fixed on the witness. "Dr. Omen, what is a criminalist?"

The doctor leans back in the seat before reacting to Taylor. "A criminalist is usually someone with special training in criminology, particularly interested in things related to crime scene investigation, evidence collection, and analysis." He wonders where this line of questioning is going.

"Is it common for a criminalist to preserve bloodstain evidence if it's available?" Taylor cautiously questions Dr. Omen, anticipating the prosecution's objection but hoping the judge will allow it.

The prosecutor jumps to his feet, "Objection, Your Honor; beyond the scope of questioning!"

"Be careful, Counselor." Judge Crane cautions her.

Taylor seeks clarity from the judge because she knows she's walking a fine line. "Your Honor, do you require I call him another day?"

Judge Crane addresses the prosecution and defense with obvious disdain. "Counselors, approach." Taylor and Mr. Robinson approach the bench, awaiting a directive.

The judge instructs, covering his microphone to keep the discussion inconspicuous. "I will follow the rules to the letter of the law in this case. And if I must, I will err on the side of caution. Ms. Alexander, I won't tolerate any tactics."

Taylor doesn't know what he meant by tactics, but she does not want to get on the judge's wrong side. "Yes, Your Honor." He gives her a look of warning before saying, "Now proceed." Mr. Robinson goes back to the prosecution's table while Taylor takes a few steps to the witness stand. She faces the jury and persists. "One final question, Dr. Omen. Did the victim have burn injuries?"

Dr. Omen is puzzled. "No, no burn injuries."

"No further questions. Thank you, Dr. Omen." Taylor resumes her seat next to Boyd at the defense's table.

Looking at the time of day, Judge Crane addresses the Court. "We will reconvene at 9:00 a.m. tomorrow."

After the courtroom clears, Taylor and Hansen assure Boyd the trial is progressing as expected. The prosecution provided no concrete evidence against Boyd. Hansen recaps the defense provided enough evidence to cause reasonable doubt. Isaiah listens closely as Taylor and Hansen discuss the next day with Boyd. Mr. Rollins is the defense's next witness. His testimony paves the way to thorough questioning regarding burn injuries.

She and Hansen grab an early dinner to prepare for tomorrow. Besides, she wants details on Hansen's date. And Dulaney arrives later in the evening. Her concert is tomorrow night, and Taylor's apprehensive about Dulaney performing is in full effect. It's almost 9:00 p.m. when she and Hansen finish their working dinner. He joins Amy for a nightcap. They hit it off since meeting in the corridors of the courthouse annex.

Taylor listens to jazz with a glass of wine and chocolates waiting for Dulaney, who didn't share information on her accommodations. Apparently, she drifted off because when she raised her head from the uncomfortable pillow on the sofa, the clock read 1:15 a.m. She never put the docking station back in the bedroom since Isaiah moved it. There are no messages from Dulaney on her phone. Taylor presses the speed dial for Dulaney. An unfamiliar voice answers, "Ms. Smith's phone."

"Who is this?" The concern in Taylor's voice is more than apparent.

"This is Jaz."

"May I speak with Dulaney, please?" Taylor isn't asking.

Oblivious to the contempt in Taylor's voice, Jaz counters. "She is in sound check. I can have her call you."

"Sound check? Where? Never mind; have her call me." At least Taylor knows Dulaney made it to Los Angeles safely. She will pluck her on the forehead for being inconsiderate when she sees her. They used to do that to each other when they were kids. For now, Taylor crawls under the soft covers of the bed. When she places her phone on the nightstand, she notices a voicemail from Isaiah. She presses listen, and his husky voice boasts through the speaker. Hi, Counselor. You are beautiful. Your very presence says, love. I am uncertain why you won't talk to me, but I pray you will. Goodnight. Taylor goes to bed smiling.

On Thursday morning, the defense calls Mr. Rollins of the Santa Monica Mountains Conservancy. Judge Crane reminds Mr. Rollins he is still under oath and instructs Taylor to proceed with her examination.

Taylor rises from her chair and marches to the witness stand. "Good morning, Mr. Rollins. Does the Santa Monica Mountains Conservancy employ you?"

Mr. Rollins is a polite older man, and his response reflects his mannerisms. "Yes, ma'am; I am."

His gentleness is contagious, causing Taylor's demeanor to soften as she continues her cross-examination. "And how long have you held this job?"

"26 years," the pride and joy ooze from Mr. Rollins in his tone and his body language.

"Will you tell the jury in what capacity, Mr. Rollins?"

Mr. Rollins does not hesitate. He takes pride in his job. "I am in charge of managing the preservation of land. I work with the National Park Service and the California State Parks."

Stepping closer, within a few feet of Mr. Rollins, "The Santa Monica Mountains have dry, warm to humid summers; is that correct?"

With no reluctance, "Yes."

Taylor segues to the issue of wildfires. "And is it true that in the summer, the climate is dry?"

"Yes, that is correct." Mr. Rollins confidently answers. He is comfortable with her questions.

Taylor is deliberate in her choice of words. "Will the dry climate make the range prone to wildfires?

"Yes, ma'am, it would."

"Do you recall if there were wildfires in the mountains on or about September 7th?" Taylor waits. This is a pivotal point in her cross-examination. She scans the jury and awaits Mr. Rollins' reply.

After a moment where he outwardly recollects, Mr. Rollins resolves. "I need to check my register, ma'am. I don't commit that information to memory." He scratches his head, trying to search his memory.

Taylor saunters to the defense table, gathers a piece of paper, and turns back to the judge's bench. She hands the judge the paper, who observes, okays it, and returns it to Taylor. "Your Honor, the defense moves to introduce as Exhibit 101 the register from the Santa Monica Mountains Conservancy."

Judge Crane returns, "The Court will receive Exhibit 101."

"Thank you, Your Honor." Taylor strides to the prosecution table and hands a copy of Exhibit 101 to the prosecuting attorney. Returning to the witness and handing him a copy of Exhibit 101, "Mr. Rollins, are there wildfires logged on or about September 7th?" She is patient as he examines the register.

After scanning the register Taylor presented him, Mr. Rollins looks up at her. "Not on the exact date, ma'am, but there is one logged a few days before." He's not sure what to do with the register, so he reaches it back to her.

She doesn't accept it but gestures to it and asks him, "Will you tell the jury the date, Mr. Rollins?"

He skims the register again, searching for the line he just viewed. When he locates it, he replies without looking up, afraid he'll lose the spot. "Yes, ma'am. It is on September 5th." He looks up when Taylor asks her next question, placing the register on the ledge.

Standing in front of the jury, Taylor addresses the witness. "September 5th." She repositions, gleaning a better view of the jury. "Mr. Rollins, would the land be hot on September 7th if there was a wildfire on September 5th?"

Before Mr. Rollins answered, the prosecutor interjected. "Objection! The witness is not qualified to answer!" He hopes the judge grants his objection.

"He's your expert, Counselor. Overruled." The judge bows to Taylor as affirmation she can resume.

"Mr. Rollins, if there were a wildfire on September 5th, would the land be hot on September 7th?"

"Yes, ma'am. If I may explain..." Mr. Rollins looks to the judge and back to Taylor, awaiting confirmation before he leans forward to explain. "You see, a wildfire is an uncontrolled fire in an area of combustible vegetation fueled by weather, wind, and dry underbrush. It differs from other fires by its size, sometimes its speed and even skips surfaces, like roads and rivers." Mr. Rollins is satisfied with his explanation and sits back on the stand.

"Mr. Rollins, I'd like to clarify, fueled by the weather. Would that include dry climate?" She stands attentively and waits for Mr. Rollins' confirmation.

"Oh, yes, ma'am. Here in California, the hot, dry winds exacerbate wildfires. They carry a spark for miles in minutes."

"Thank you, Mr. Rollins. Nothing further."

As Taylor takes her chair, the prosecutor asks, "Mr. Rollins, exactly how many days does it take before the underbrush cools?"

"I cannot say exactly, sir. It depends."

"Depends on what?" the prosecutor persists.

"Several factors, but mainly the suppression method. Firefighters fight wildfires by depriving them of fuel, oxygen, or heat." Mr. Rollins sticks to facts in his explanation.

Standing behind the prosecution table, fumbling at a pen in hand, "Do you recall the suppression method used on the wildfire on September 5th logged on Exhibit 101?"

"No, sir. We do not record those details."

"What are typical suppression methods, Mr. Rollins? Could it be water dousing?" the prosecutor tries to taint the defense's theory.

Mr. Rollins faces the jury as he explains. "Wildfire suppression depends on the technologies available. And yes, water dousing is one method. Firefighters also deliberately start fires in a process called controlled burning."

Regretting he asked, the prosecutor interrupts his witness's explanation. "Thank you, Mr. Rollins." Looking at the judge bemused, "Your Honor, the prosecution rests."

Remaining seated, Taylor asks, "Mr. Rollins, one last question. Does it take more than 48 hours for the land to cool?"

"Yes, ma'am. It takes days before the underbrush cools."

"Thank you, Mr. Rollins. Nothing further."

Judge Crane instructs, "Mr. Rollins, you may step down. We will hear closing statements when the Court reconvenes at 1:00 p.m."

Taylor and Hansen join Boyd, Isaiah, and Mayor Sellect for a quick lunch. The Mayor teases Taylor, "I hear you're giving my nephew a hard time." Taylor is embarrassed, and her flush face reveals it. As if knowing her best friend needs rescuing, Dulaney's face appears on Taylor's phone as it vibrates. "Excuse me, gentlemen. I need to take this."

Taylor answers without a greeting. "Dulaney Renee Smith. Where are you? Why didn't you call me last night?" Dulaney recognizes the misdirected frustration. Understanding the pressure of trial, Dulaney does not snap back at Taylor.

"Tay, relax. I'm at The Westin, suite 2505. It was 3:00 a.m. when we finished sound check. Why wake you?" Dulaney gives Taylor a moment to interrogate. "I delivered your VIP pass and the clothes from your closet to your suite."

Relieved but not letting up, "Why were you in sound check so late?" Taylor was protective of Dulaney since third grade, but particularly in the last two years.

Dulaney speculates something other than the trail bothers Taylor. She knows her friend, and this tone isn't her usual. "My treatment was this morning, and you know I need to rest afterward. And, I want to catch the afternoon of your trial. Those two activities didn't support an afternoon sound check. What time do you go back?" Dulaney remains unruffled, bringing her friend's blood pressure back to normal.

"We reconvene at 1:00 p.m." Defeat is in Taylor's voice. Dulaney will pry later; right now, Taylor needs to focus on the trial.

"I'll be in the back of the courtroom. And Tay..."

"Yes?"

"Thank you for your unwavering friendship." With that, Dulaney hangs up. She doesn't need Taylor to get all schmaltzy. Taylor turns on the ball of her feet into Isaiah. How long was he standing there? How much of her conversation did he hear?

"Taylor, why are you avoiding me?" Isaiah touches Taylor's elbow, but she steps back. "Let it be, Isaiah. Just leave it alone." Taylor can't answer his question. She is embarrassed—ashamed, maybe—because she lost her virginity to a stranger. Admittedly, she felt something, but she didn't dissect her feelings. Her focus is on keeping her client—his brother—out of prison.

"Taylor, what does that mean?" The plea in Isaiah's voice is real. He struggles to manage his emotions. Isaiah shocks her by calling her by name. He always addresses her as Counselor, but not these two times. She doesn't object to him calling her Counselor because he makes it sound like a melody. "It means we'll accept what happened for what it is—lust. Now leave it alone." Taylor steps forward, but Isaiah keeps talking.

"You can't tell me I am placating. I am in love with you, and I think deep down you love me too." Isaiah confesses his emotions.

Did he just say he is in love with her? She has closing arguments in less than an hour. "Isaiah, let me get through closing arguments, please?" Taylor is adamant the trial takes precedence. She detected a miscue during direct examination when her thoughts wandered to Isaiah's voicemails. Focus Taylor, a man's life is at stake.

She practiced her closing statement repeatedly, but now considers Hansen delivering closing statements. Shaking her head to clear her thoughts of Isaiah, Taylor walks back to the table where the others are finishing lunch. "Hansen, we should get back. Mr. Myers, we'll see you back in the courtroom at 12:45 p.m."

"I thought the Judge said 1 o'clock?"

"He did, but we say 12:45 p.m." Hansen reiterates Taylor's instruction and rises from his seat. He and Taylor walk back to the courthouse in silence.

Dulaney slides into the back of the courtroom as the prosecutor delivers his closing statement. Taylor doesn't see her, but she promised to be there, and she is. Taylor prays silently, Father, you are all knowing and ever-present. This man sits next to me, pleading his innocence before the jury and this Court. But Father, I ask you to be the judge and jury. You know this man's fate. You know the verdict. Let justice prevail, and your will be done. In Jesus' name, I pray. Amen. Taylor hears the prosecutor addressing the jury.

"If it pleases the Court, ladies and gentlemen of the jury, thank you. You paid extreme attention through this arduous process, and I am appreciative. After we complete closing statements, the judge will turn this case over to you to complete your service. I need you to understand the defendant stands before you and this Court accused of a crime. Recognize through the history of this world, it is unlawful to take—and attempt to take—another's life. You sat through the proceedings; you saw and heard the evidence. Now I ask you to consider this. How can you act in good faith and attempt to take the life of a human being? We believe the facts prove beyond a reasonable doubt the defendant acted with depraved indifference. And now, I respectfully request you return a verdict of guilty. Thank you, ladies and gentlemen."

Taylor observes the courtroom as the prosecution ends its closing statement. It is silent; you can hear a pin drop. But the jury looks indifferent. She made her case; presented enough facts to prove reasonable doubt. She said a prayer, believing God to show mercy on her client. Now it is her time to close strong. The prosecutor takes his seat, and Taylor rises from hers. She stands directly in front of and greets the jury, "One would need to be either homicidal or suicidal to attempt the life of a police officer. Boyd Myers is neither. He told you he did not shoot Detective Franklin, nor did he leave the detective's body in the mountains. The evidence supports this. Boyd Myers does not own a gun. His fingerprints were not found at the crime scene. The airline and hotel receipts verified his presence in Maui. You saw the pictures on the day the detective was shot. Surveillance tapes show Mr. Myers entering his building on September 7th—the day they allegedly found the detective in the mountains. Surveillance also shows he didn't leave again until the next morning. The prosecution found no weapon. Their evidence is purely circumstantial. Recall the medical examiner testified there were no burn injuries on Detective Franklin's body. And Mr. Rollins affirmed it takes several days for the land to cool after a forest fire. According to expert testimony, if Detective Franklin lay in the summit for 48 hours, as the prosecution would have you believe, his body or some parts of his body would be scalded. Tragically, someone attempted to take Detective Franklin's life. But Boyd Myers is not your assassin. The suspect is still out there. So I ask, after you evaluate the evidence, to return a verdict of not guilty. Thank you, ladies and gentlemen."

Judge Crane announces Court reconvenes at 9:00 a.m. He will instruct the jury then. He wraps his gavel against the bench, and Court adjourns.

The timing is good and bad. It is late afternoon. Presumably, the judge doesn't want jury deliberation beginning close to 5:00 p.m. Taylor asks Hansen, "How do you feel, Counselor?" They laugh at her teasing him by calling him, Counselor.

"I predict a not guilty verdict." Hansen is convinced the prosecution failed to provide concrete evidence to convict. They talk with Boyd and advise him on ways to relax this evening. Taylor looks up and sees Dulaney in the back row. Simultaneously, Dulaney texts Taylor, *excellent job, Tay*! Taylor laughs, and a thought pops into her head. "Hansen, would you like to join me at a neo/soul concert tonight?"

"Are you asking me on a date?" Hansen pesters Taylor. "Sure. Where? Who?"

Taylor points to Dulaney in the back of the courtroom, "See that young lady back there?" Before she finishes, Hansen exclaims, "That is Dulaney Smith—one of the best neo/soul artists alive." He wreaks excitement. "Does she know the Myers?"

Taylor doesn't bother bantering him, given the sheer joy on his face. He worked long, hard hours preparing for the trial. The concert is a pleasant way for him to unwind. "She is my best friend." Hansen is beside himself. "Your best friend? That Dulaney Smith is your best friend?" Hansen enunciates each word to make sure Taylor understands him.

"Yes, she is. Want to meet her?" Taylor dare not torment him, given his sheer joy. He is clearly a fan.

"Don't joke, Taylor." Hansen turns into a high-school boy about to meet his girl crush.

"Come," Taylor says as she picks up her bag. Isaiah stands a few feet away while waiting for her. She approaches him with Hansen on her heels, ecstatic to meet Dulaney. "I waited for you to get through the closing statement—which was very good, by the way. You are a natural in the courtroom. Have dinner with me?"

The words escape her lips without aforethought. "Why don't you join me at Dulaney's concert at Staples Center tonight."

Isaiah is first shocked Taylor is going to the concert, and second, she could get tickets. "That show is sold out. Boyd tried to get tickets."

Taylor badgers, "Let's ask Dulaney if she has extras. I see her back there." Taylor points toward her best friend. Dulaney flings a slick wave at Taylor, appreciating the crowd might be fans.

"Do you know her?" Isaiah peers back & forth from Taylor to Dulaney.

"She is my best friend." Isaiah is as speechless as Hansen, who stands next to Taylor in disbelief. "Would you like to go to the show? Let me see if it's alright if your brother joins too."

Taylor meets Dulaney, who's shimmying toward her and her fans. "Tay, you're good." Dulaney encourages her friend and absorbs her in a bear hug.

"I can't breathe, D," and Dulaney releases Taylor from her grips. Hansen and Isaiah trail on Taylor's heels. "Dulaney, this is my colleague, Hansen, and this is Isaiah Myers." Taylor points out the men to Dulaney, who greets them with handshakes. Taylor bids, "Do you mind if they join me in VIP tonight?" Remembering Boyd, Taylor adds, "Oh, and Isaiah's brother needs access."

Dulaney calls Jaz, "We need three reserves in VIP. They're friends of Tay." Dulaney ends her call with, "Great; see you shortly." Dulaney excites her fans with, "All done." Taylor hugs her again in gratitude.

"Thank you so much, Ms. Smith," Hansen extends his hand to shake hers again.

"My pleasure," she shakes Hansen's hand a second time. "Tay, I have to go. Do you have time to walk with me to the hotel?"

"Yup!" She tells Hansen, "Meet you in the hotel lobby at 6:40 p.m." In a softer tone, she extends an olive branch to Isaiah, "Hotel lobby at 6:15 p.m.? Let's get a drink before the show."

"See you at 6:15 p.m.," Isaiah hugs Taylor, thanks Dulaney, and departs the courtroom to catch up with Boyd. Hansen follows, mischievously pointing fingers at Taylor. Dulaney and Taylor head for the exit, "What did I miss back there?" Dulaney ask.

"Nothing, D. Catch me up on you." Taylor quickly switches gears. "What made you get back on stage? How do you feel? You mentioned a treatment this morning." Dulaney bumps Taylor against her shoulder, admiring her. Taylor's interrogating started in third grade, and today is no different.

"Let's see. My best friend left me after harshly telling me to get it together. Did I mention it was one day after the man who I can't get out of my system ran out on me? After I cried a river..." they laugh hard, suspending Dulaney's dramatic rationalization. "As I said, after I cried a river, I meditated and prayed continuously. God said He never told me to stop living, and I should get back to it. After that confirmation, I went to the studio and gave everyone a heart attack when I walked in. I stepped into the booth and released my emotions. It was cleansing." Taylor is proud Dulaney reacquainted herself with her music.

By this time, Taylor and Dulaney reach the hotel. They are both on the 25th floor. Dulaney joins Taylor in her suite to finish catching up. Other than the time Taylor spent in Asia, they were never in separate states for this long. Taylor hands Dulaney a bottle of water and asks, "D, can I ask you something?"

"Sure." Dulaney knows Taylor is concerned about her jumping back into the mix. And she loves her for it. But the exhilaration of her music gives her life. It is unparalleled. But Taylor cut Dulaney off at the knees with her question.

"When will you face your truths with Coltrane? You know he loves you." Dulaney is prepared for Taylor's meddling about her health, moving too fast, performing. But she brings up Coltrane. Taylor knows how to piss Dulaney off effortlessly, and by the look on Dulaney's face, she did.

Dulaney's trembling, "Taylor, don't interfere."

In a way only Taylor knows how; she pushes. "Why do you clam up when it comes to him? Why won't you forgive him?" There are things about Coltrane Taylor doesn't know. Those details affect Dulaney's relationship with Coltrane. Yes, the three of them were inseparable since third grade—

until recent years. She isn't sure why Coltrane never told Taylor, but it isn't her story to tell. She pleads, "Taylor, let it rest!" Taylor doesn't listen.

Dulaney recalls the day to the hour and minute when she and Coltrane crossed the lines of friendship. He always loved her, but it wasn't until she saw them as a family with children she entertained his advances. She fasted and prayed until she had a clear response from God. Dulaney is shaken from her thoughts with Taylor's pressing. "What is it? It can't be that bad!" And Dulaney explodes.

"My truth—live in my truth, you say—here's my truth." Dulaney is furious, and in that fury, she yells, "Coltrane is married!" Taylor can't believe her ears. "It's his secret, and while he says it's a marriage of convenience, it's marriage. Add salt to the wound—I'm in love with him. And while he says he and his wife accept it's a marriage of convenience, there are twin girls who give him life. That's your friend's secret, Taylor!" Dulaney pauses only slightly to catch her breath.

"Deal with it and stop running, you say. Well, Tay, running is how I deal with it. I run to my music, pouring my emotions into every lyric. It's out of order in God's eyes. And we justify our wrongdoings with two thoughts: one, we're only human, and two; it's better to have loved than not." If it isn't apparent in Dulaney's voice, her struggle becomes real as her yell turns into a whimper. "Make matters worse, you already know I have cancer, and I can't tell him because it'll destroy him. While I believe wholeheartedly there's healing in the blood, I don't know God's plan for this thing. So yes, I run. I run because if running from the man I love will cause God to give me a longer life, then that's a decision I can accept and, how d'you put—deal with it."

Dulaney peers through her tears as she gasps. "That's my truth, Tay—so pardon me if my dealing with it does not suit your liking. Ask your friend why he never told you his secret. Now I've got a show to prepare for." Dulaney leaves Taylor in a sheer shudder.

What does she mean Coltrane is married? Taylor weeps. Twin girls—wow! Shock and confusion overwhelm her. Her first instinct is to run after Dulaney, but her legs won't move. She will talk with her when she's not within hours of a sold-out concert. Never did she intend to upset Dulaney? Taylor sat in incredulity for some time before meeting Isaiah & Hansen.

Taylor saunters into the hotel's bar at 6:20 p.m. to find Isaiah sipping on a beer. She didn't know he likes beer. A glass of Cab awaited her, but she desired a Cosmo. She riled her best friend—mind you, a short time before she takes the stage. She and Isaiah exchange small talk, nothing heavy. Hansen arrives promptly at 6:40 p.m., and they make their way to the Staples Center, where they meet Boyd at the entrance.

The concert is a blast. The arena sold out, earning the Atlanta diva the best reviews of her career. Dulaney is undeniably in her element on stage. Amid a life-altering illness, Dulaney announces tour dates, including concerts in Anaheim, San Antonio, New Orleans, Philadelphia, and back by popular demand, Atlanta. Dulaney assures her fans an unforgettable experience, offering something for everyone—a blend of R&B mixed with neo-soul. True to form, she sings Amazing Grace as she exits the stage. The announcement of tour dates shakes Taylor to her core, but she will support her friend on tour. First, she has a man to keep out of prison.

When Boyd arrives at the courthouse the next morning, the crowd outside is unbelievable. People with signs—some supporters, some not—yelling. News reporters line the steps of the courthouse. He fights through the crowd, avoiding the media. Once inside, he paces the stone floor outside the courtroom—his anxiety is increasingly gaining strength. It's as if a hurricane is tearing through his life, leaving nothing to salvage. There isn't an empty seat in the courtroom. Taylor and Hansen are seated at their table. He acknowledges them when he approaches, and Taylor discerns his anguish. Fear emits from Boyd.

The judge calls the Court to order with a single wrap of his gavel. He briefs the jury and confirms that each member understands, educating them on the relevant laws to guide their deliberations. After reviewing the issues in the case, he defines unfamiliar terms. The standard of proof the jurors apply to the case is evaluated—beyond a reasonable doubt. Lastly, the judge advises they are to consider the facts and credibility of witnesses and base their conclusion on the trial's evidence. He dismisses the jury for deliberations.

After the jury box empties and the courtroom clears, Hansen leans forward, looking past Boyd to gain Taylor's attention. "Want to head to the office while the jury is retired." Taylor stuffs manila envelopes in her crossover and nods in agreement. Boyd looks to Taylor, confused.

Giving her attention to her client, Taylor explains. "The Judge will probably hear motions while the jury deliberates. You can wait in our office." Boyd meekly shakes his head. The pressure and anxiety are ostensible.

Taylor leads the way to the office, with Boyd and Hansen following. Boyd strolls, absorbing the fresh air, wondering if this is the last time he walks freely along the streets of downtown Los Angeles. The thought sickens him. He is innocent yet may go to jail for attempted murder.

Walking alongside Taylor, Hansen thanks her for the show. His delight in meeting Dulaney is still evident. "Ooh, thank you again for the concert. It was awesome."

"You are welcome, Counselor."

Taylor's reference to him as Counselor pleases him. It infers she trusts him as her law partner. He jokes, "I see somebody is rubbing off on you." They laugh. "What's the deal, anyway? It seems there is tension between you two."

Hansen's questions remind her she has to talk with Isaiah, but not today. Taylor notices Boyd's linger as they approach the building but doesn't call attention to it. She slows her stride for him to catch up. "Am I on trial?" He throws his hands up in defeat.

Mr. Daniels and the mayor are exchanging stories when they arrive. Before Hansen or Taylor speaks, the Mayor asks, "What's your read on the jury?"

To be honest, this jury was hard to read. She leans against the window and focuses on the two gentlemen. "We made our selections based on key values and viewpoints during voir dire." Why did she explain the voir dire process since four of the six people in the room are lawyers?

The Mayor firmly observes Taylor, wondering why she sidestepped his question. "How much time do you predict they'll deliberate?"

Gazing randomly around the room, "No predictions; we'll wait and see." She rises from the window where she leans. "I'll be in my office if anyone needs me." She exits the conference room. As she walks down the corridor, she visualizes the poker faces of the twelve jurors. They were hard to read.

Staring out the office window, Taylor contemplates. From Dulaney's words repeatedly echoing to the jurors' apathetic faces, to Isaiah—her thoughts consume her. A man's fate rests on how well she conveyed evidence and convinced the jury of his innocence. It's enough she must deal with Isaiah; she does not need secrets from her friends. She regrets mentioning Coltrane to Dulaney but has so many questions. And she excels in the line of questioning.

The red light blinks on the desk phone. Taylor presses it. When Isaiah's voice echoes through the speaker, she closes the door.

I want to satisfy your every single need, Counselor; listen to every word you say. I want to know you in every way. Since rescuing you from the balcony, my only desire is to please you. Give me a chance to make you smile and make that smile last for a long while.

The message is beautiful. It sounds like a love song. She listens to Isaiah's messages—he left one every day—and each one is even more beautiful than the previous.

Counselor, it's my mission to satisfy you. After that night, you are all I think of. You are now a part of my soul. Don't run away from me. Talk to me, Taylor.

Let's sit and talk it over. It's not lust; it's love. I hurt every day you won't talk to me.

The last voice mail Isaiah left was last night after Dulaney's concert. He said I had a wonderful time, Counselor. Your friend is very talented. Goodnight. It sounds final. Taylor will talk to him after the verdict. Absentmindedly, she dials Isaiah. "Counselor," he picks up on the second ring.

"Hi," Taylor mumbles. His beautiful messages hypnotized her.

It isn't clear if her call is about Boyd or their relationship. Until the concert, she hadn't spoken to him since brunch that Sunday. Her unusual behavior has him walking on eggshells. "Everything okay?" There's an upswing in Isaiah's concern.

Taylor is dazed. She didn't mean to call him. "Umm, yes." Clearing the fog from her brain, she regains composure. "I listened to all your voicemails. They are beautiful. Thank you." Taylor is humbled as Isaiah ever experienced. Two words to describe her are beautifully broken.

Isaiah needs Taylor to believe him. "I mean every word of every message, Taylor." He relaxes his tone but is firm. He deliberately calls her by name for emphasis.

"Can we take one day at a time?" Taylor finds herself inarticulate. Her voice trembles. Rarely is she lost for words, but presently she wades in those waters.

Relieved, Isaiah soothes her. "Yes, we can." Never did he imagine he'd fall in love with her. Since the Mayor's ball in Atlanta, he's known he wanted to get to know the sharpshooter he met on the balcony. "And Counselor..."

"Yes?" Taylor's daze prohibits her. She cannot form intelligent sentences.

"Will you promise to communicate with me?" Isaiah begs.

There is a silence, but not one of those awkward ones. It's as though they're interacting in silence. Taylor regains consciousness and the strength in her voice. "I can do that," she comforts Isaiah. "We'll talk later."

He smiles, and he is sure she senses it. "I'll hold you to that. Bye, Counselor."

"Bye." A smile warms Taylor's face, and she hangs up. She notices Hansen at the door and motions for him to enter.

"I couldn't read the jury. At one point, I thought we—well, you—persuaded them. But man, they had poker faces." Hansen blurts out as he takes a seat. "What do you think?"

"They were not an easy jury to read."

In his usual up-tempo voice and waving his hands in no particular way, "All we can do is wait." Hansen gets up from the chair he sat in minutes ago. Taylor observes his body language and concludes he has nervous energy. "Do you need anything? I'm going to run out for a minute."

"Not far, right?" Taylor raises an eyebrow. She wants everyone near when the Clerk alerts of the jury's return.

As if reading her mind, "No, not far. I'll be closer than you if they call in five minutes." Taylor knows he's going to see Amy. Neither she nor Hansen thought about a pass for Amy for the concert. "I'm going to surprise Amy with her favorite macchiato. You want something?"

"That's sweet of you; I'm fine." As Hansen disappears from the doorway, Taylor calls to him, "Check on your client before you run off to play night in shining armor."

Hansen hears Taylor's squeal and backs up enough to peek in the doorway, "I did. But the Mayor is lecturing him, so he's occupied."

This triggers the memory of the Mayor's comment of the brothers' difference. "Really? About the case?"

"Couldn't tell. He stopped talking when I entered the room. You want me to find out?" he inquires.

"Yes, but after you show off your kindness." Taylor shoos Hansen out of her office. She doesn't want him en route either to or from the courthouse when the jury returns. Hansen is thrilled with his budding relationship and shows his care for Amy through simple acts of thoughtfulness. "See you in a bit." This time Hansen pauses for last-minute requests before heading to the elevator.

Taylor waves off Hansen and turns to her computer. She responds to emails from The Foundation and makes calls for donations of computers. Afraid to mention the news Dulaney sprung on her, she avoids calling the Center. She can't stop thinking Coltrane has a wife and twins. That is undoubtedly not a conversation to have over the phone. When she finishes with emails, she marks Dulaney's tour dates on her calendar, although not thrilled with Dulaney's decision to tour.

Hansen places her favorite tea on the desk without a word. She didn't hear him walk in but is glad he's back. She'll miss Hansen when she returns to Atlanta. They formed a unique bond. While she tries her best to adhere to Philippians 4:6, she is anxious for the verdict.

Jury deliberation endures. They took the exhibits and the judge's instructions to the jury room. To Taylor's knowledge, there is no request for clarification or questions about the evidence. The jury has only to choose the proper verdict form when they reach a decision, but the verdict must be unanimous. Is there one who was not persuaded? Did she not win the pivotal point with all the jurors and removed the doubt?

Late afternoon, Taylor is disturbed from her thoughts by Hansen's tap on her office door. "No verdict, but the Judge wants to see us in his chambers."

CHAPTER 6

The Verdict

Is the jury deadlocked?

Taylor asks Hansen, "Did you inform Boyd?"

"No." Hansen thinks Taylor will deliver the news.

"Meet me in the conference room." Hansen's slow walk to the conference room gives him time to wonder why the judge called them. He also considers Boyd, whose anxiety intensified with every waiting hour.

Everyone gathers at the table when Taylor walks into the room. Mr. Daniels speaks first. "Any news, Ms. Alexander?" Taylor faces Boyd. "The Judge summoned us to his chambers. I do not know why; his clerk did not give details." Boyd's shock renders him silent. All hope evaporates from his body. Taylor resumes, "Let's say a prayer before we go to the courthouse."

The Mayor exclaims, "What do you mean you don't know why?" Taylor is mindful of the nervousness in the room as she responds. "I do not know why the Judge asked to see us, and honestly, I prefer not to speculate." She reaches for Boyd's hand to ask for the only help she knows—God. Unexpectedly, the Mayor leads the prayer.

The law clerk directs Taylor and Hansen to Judge Crane's chambers but asks Boyd to wait outside the door. Boyd's edgy and exclaims to the clerk, "It's my life! Why do I have to stay out?" Immediately turning to his lawyers, desperately searching for answers, "Taylor, what's happening?" Taylor gestures to the law clerk; she needs a minute with her client.

"Let us find out why the Judge asked us here." Her effort to calm Boyd fails, but she assures him it's safe to wait in the hallway. Boyd is anxious. He paces back and forth in the small vestibule while he waits.

Mr. Robinson and Hansen occupied the seats opposite the desk when Taylor joined them. Greeting the judge, "Your Honor," he motions for her to take a seat. The three lawyers sit before the judge like they are in the principal's office awaiting their reprimand. Noticing their uncomfortable demeanors, Judge Crane opens. "The jury requested information regarding the wildfires and the condition of the land on Sept 7th." Taylor thought, this isn't unusual—the jury asking for clarifying information is standard. Examining their faces, he continues. "It's past 4:00 p.m. on Friday. I am debating whether to provide the information and allow the jury as much time as necessary or reconvene deliberation on Monday morning." He waits to give the lawyers time to react. When all three remained quiet, he polls them. "What is your position, Mr. Robinson? And yours, Ms. Alexander?"

Taylor looks to Mr. Robinson as if to say; you go first. Surprisingly, Hansen inserts before either speak. "If you dismiss the jury, there's the propensity for outside opinions to contaminate them." He looks to Taylor for backup, but she remains quiet—appears to be deliberating with herself.

Mr. Robinson asks, "Will you sequester them?" Before answering Mr. Robinson, Judge Crane turns to Taylor, "Ms. Alexander, are you weighing in?" Taylor is preoccupied with forethought. She responds, "Not yet, Your Honor."

"Since Ms. Alexander does not have an opinion—." Taylor hastily stops Judge Crane as she concludes her internal judiciousness. "Oh, but I do have a perspective. I advise you to provide the jury with whatever they requested, sequester them, and reconvene on Monday." Scanning Hansen and Mr. Robinson's looks before turning to Judge Crane, "I do not recommend letting the jury go home. In that case, I strongly suggest we wait it out." Mr. Robinson concurs.

Judge Crane motions for his law clerk, "Let's gather the details for the jury and follow the sequester procedures." She collects papers from the corner of the judge's desk and exits. Boyd's pacing abruptly stops when he sees the judge's clerk. He expected to see Taylor and Hansen behind her. When he doesn't, his facial expression speaks volumes. The law clerk comforts him, "They'll be out in a few minutes." Boyd opens his mouth to say thank you, but no words come out—he is lifeless.

After a short while, the lawyers and the judge emerged from the closed door. Boyd is frightened—he doesn't know what to think or feel, or say. Taylor senses his energy and asks the judge for permission to consult with her client in his chambers. Judge Crane okays it. Taylor and Hansen explain to Boyd the jury's request for information regarding the wildfires. They reassure him it is a good sign. The jury presumably believes testimony regarding the fires' scorching ground and the doctor's testimony of no burn injuries. They explain the sequester procedure and inform him court restarts on Monday. Boyd understands his legal teams' clarifications but becomes increasingly petrified. Taylor asks, "Do you need a minute?" Boyd is unable to speak. He needs air.

Boyd texts Isaiah on the walk back to the office. He needs his brother more than he ever has in his life. Regretting ever hurting Isaiah, he vows to spend the rest of his life righting his wrong. He believes they are on the better side of recovering their brotherhood. After losing their parents years ago, they became enemies. Isaiah wanted to sell the family home; Boyd didn't. Isaiah wanted to use his share of the profits to invest in his business, and he believed his parents wanted him to. Boyd saw things differently, wanting to hold on to the home where he grew up. So, he challenged Isaiah—and won. He moved back into the family home, leasing his downtown high-rise condo. Countless fights brewed out of settling family assets. But the most reprehensible bout occurred when Boyd slept with Nyla's mother. It's unclear if Isaiah forgives him for the indiscretion with his daughter's mother, but the brothers are on a path to healing.

Isaiah receives Boyd's text. This is the first he's heard from anyone since jury deliberations started. While the others went to Mr. Daniel's office, he went to his office to finalize a trade deal for his unruly client. Isaiah did not respond but got into his convertible and drove to S. Flowers Street. Boyd, Taylor, and Hansen enter the building as he reaches the twin tower. Honking the horn doesn't get Boyd's attention. Thoughts consume him.

Boyd is relieved when his phone vibrates, and he sees Isaiah's number on the screen. "Hey, man." Isaiah hears the distress in Boyd's voice, which gives him cause for concern. Disguising his worry, Isaiah greets his brother. "I am out front. I tried to stop you when you walked in the building."

Boyd stops, causing Taylor and Hansen to pause. "Isaiah is out front. I will go talk to him." Boyd scans Taylor and Hansen's faces as if waiting for permission.

"Some boy time with your brother is good." Taylor and Hansen continue to the elevators while Boyd heads for the front entrance. He can't recall the last time he was this happy to see Isaiah. He loosens his tie, releases the navy blue pinstriped suit coat from his shoulders, and lays it on the back seat. Once buckled in on the passenger side, all the emotions that frenzied him the past several hours gushes out like water from a dam. Isaiah rests his hand on Boyd's shoulder as Boyd releases his worries.

When Boyd gathers himself, "Shots, man." Isaiah puts the car in drive, and off they go. The perfect place is a spot on Melrose Avenue with a burlesque show. Also appealing is the dealer's choice of drinks. You tell the barkeep your mood, and your alcohol is mixed based on your described state. He and Boyd used to go there when they wanted to throw back a couple. It is that kind of evening. He'd let his Uncle know he and Boyd are hanging to reduce Boyd's tension.

The Mayor's phone alerts as Taylor and Hansen walk into the conference room—without Boyd. It's Isaiah; he will return his nephew's call after Taylor's debrief. In unison, the Mayor and Mr. Daniels ask, "Where's Boyd?" The Mayor continues without waiting for the answer, "Why did Crane beckon you?" Taylor explains the jury requested detailed information on the wildfires and the doctor's testimony regarding the absence of burns from the victim and the judge's decision to sequester the jury since it's late on Friday. Her explanation appeased the room but the Mayor probes again, "Where is Boyd?"

"He's with Isaiah." Taylor reduces the Mayor's unease and continues, "It's now 5:30 p.m. There is nothing left for us to do here today. Let's remain optimistic the jury returns on Monday with a not guilty verdict." After she encourages everyone to keep a positive outlook, she announces her departure for the day. She and Hansen exchange plans for Saturday, and they both leave.

Taylor considers an early dinner with Delaney to apologize for the commotion she caused before her show. But she's experienced her share of stress for one day. Tonight, her recipe for a relaxing evening is room service, an in-suite massage, and a martini. As Taylor enters the hotel's revolving door, a text from Isaiah pops on her phone. *Hanging with Boyd. Let's catch up tomorrow.* Her only response is a thumb's up emoji.

First is the in-suite massage, leaving the spa-type music playing to maintain the atmosphere—next, order in-room dining and a martini before showering. Sitting on the small sofa expecting her food, Taylor notices an envelope on the kitchenette countertop. As she's uncovering its contents, a knock alerts her of dinner. After the attendant sets up her cuisine, she goes back to the envelope. The note reads; Tour to Napa departs the hotel at 7:00 a.m. sharp. I'll see you at breakfast at 6:30 a.m. Sometimes she believes she doesn't deserve Delaney's friendship, which amplifies her love for her friend. This is one of those times.

When she and Delaney planned to visit Napa, Taylor didn't foresee the jury not returning a verdict today. After her blow-up on Thursday, she didn't think Delaney wanted to talk to her, let alone spend the day with her. Now, she isn't sure about visiting the vineyards since the jury is still deliberating.

She enjoyed her dinner—she always orders the same Asian salad. This time, she ordered French fries to accompany her martini. The week took its toll on her. After dinner and drink, Taylor crawls under the soft white bedsheets, setting the alarm for 6:00 a.m.

Isaiah contemplated calling, hoping she was awake. The phone vibration awakens Taylor. Incoherently answering, "Hello."

He regrets waking her. "Go back to sleep. I'll call you tomorrow." Taylor doesn't know what time it is. She isn't even sure she responded, but turns over and falls back into a restful sleep—that is, until her alarm sounds.

Before going to bed, she pondered the Napa trip but didn't confirm. When she silences the alarm, she sees two text messages—Isaiah and Delaney. The texts read, *sorry for waking you* and *looking forward to Napa*, respectively. She drags herself out of bed and into the shower.

When Taylor enters the breakfast area, Delaney is drinking coffee with a plate of fruit and ordered tea for Taylor. Taylor hugs her and slides into the booth, "Good morning, Sunshine."

Delaney returns the good morning and asks, "How did your trial end? What was the verdict?" Taylor's look changes Delaney's demeanor to empathetic. "What happened, Tay? Did you lose?"

Taylor explains the jury requested information, and the judge sequestered them, allowing discussions to progress through the weekend. "Given the state of the trial, this weekend isn't ideal for me to go to Napa. What if the judge orders us to appear again?" Taylor voices her concern.

"It'll be okay. You need to relax. And, we can catch up." Delaney's convincing doesn't resonate with Taylor, though she respects Dulaney for always looking for the silver lining. It reminds her of the first day of third grade. Taylor was upset she didn't get a front-row desk. Her father dropped her at school late. When she walked into her classroom, few seats remained. Taylor was outraged that Delaney sat in the first row across from the teacher's desk. But Delaney smiled at her. She insisted Delaney took her desk—not because she thought Delaney believed her, but because her smile said she'd be nice enough to let her have it—and she did.

Delaney notices Taylor's uneasiness and suggests, "Let's check out a local tour?" The energetic waiter who takes her order disrupts Taylor's response. She opts for the buffet.

"I am comfortable if we stay close. Do you have a vineyard in mind?" Delaney searches on her phone while Taylor selects food from the spread. By the time Taylor returns to their table, Delaney has coordinated a day trip.

"Okay, we board the X Wine Railroad at Union Station and ride along the coast to Santa Barbara. From there, a van takes us to wine country. The train leaves at 9:00 a.m."

The train ride alongside the Pacific coast is incredible, from the vintage rail cars, tons of food selections, and the splendid views of the Pacific Ocean. A walk-through of the winery and vineyard is splendid. The guide moves to the estate tasting after topping off the tour with a champagne toast. Cheeses, nuts, and chocolate complement the flight of five wines. It is by far one of the best tastings ever. Taylor and Delaney don't participate in the wine crawl. In place of, they order a charcuterie board with glasses of their favorite wine from the flight and chill on the grounds.

Delaney interrupts their silence. She knows the news of Coltrane's marriage stupefied Taylor; she clears the air. "Tay, I am sorry for lashing out at you the other night--" Taylor cuts off Delaney's apology. "No, D, I apologize! I pressed long after you asked me to stop." Taylor lets her words lag because it's hazy whether Delaney will expound. Coltrane's news not only surprised her; but also offended her. The two people she's closest to disappointed her by withholding such intimate details. She is clueless about why or how long.

Hurt emanates from Taylor's tone. It also coats her face. While Dulaney strongly believed this was Coltrane's story to tell, she enlightens Taylor. "When you were in Asia, before Coltrane and I crossed friendship lines, he dated a girl in Charlotte—not serious at first. She stopped dating him after he shared he didn't want children." Delaney sipped her wine, giving Taylor time to process before she continued. "Three years ago, he learns the girl died giving birth to twin girls—his twin girls."

Taylor is flabbergasted. "Three years ago. That aligns with y'all demise. Is this why?"

"At first, I didn't know; neither did he. I was upset because I thought he stood me up on my birthday. When he called two days later, naturally, I ignored him."

"Wait, he found out on your birthday?" Taylor connects events.

"The hospital called him, and he hurried to Charlotte. He was her emergency contact."

This is too much for Taylor. "Why is Coltrane her emergency contact?"

145

"Taylor, I have no idea. Anyway, he took care of her burial, and her friend cared for the twin babies."

"Where is her family?"

"He said the foster system raised her." Dulaney relives painful memories.

"How does he discover the twin girls are his?"

Delaney continues. "The girl's friend adopted the twins. A year later, she finds a sealed letter addressed to Coltrane in her friends' memories. She mails it to him, and it reveals Coltrane is the father. A DNA test confirmed paternity."

How did all this go on in her friends' lives without her knowledge? "Why did you keep this from me, D?" Taylor's hurt is unmistakable.

Delaney compassionately places her hand on top of Taylor's, "It wasn't mine to tell."

"But—" Taylor cannot articulate words as tears covered her cheeks. "You are my friends, my family." She wipes her cheek with the back of her hand. "Why didn't he want me to know? Is this why you don't talk to him?" Tears stream uncontrollably down Taylor's face.

"In part." While the deceased's friend asked nothing of Coltrane, he wants to know his children. Initially, he asked for visitation, which the friend refused. The friend, now the twins' adopted mother, was afraid he'd take them. After many unsuccessful attempts to remedy this, Coltrane hired an attorney who recommended mediation. It was during mediation where it's suggested Coltrane marries the adopted mother. He couldn't overturn the adoption; it was final. As farfetched as it was, Coltrane married a stranger so he can raise his children. That, and let's not forget his infidelity, forced Dulaney to walk away. "He promised to tell you." Delaney couldn't defend Coltrane. The truth is, she does not know why he keeps this from Taylor. Delaney moves to the side of the makeshift blanket and hugs her friend.

They enjoy the rest of their time at the vineyard pairing wines, swapping stories, and taking in the experience. "I have something to tell you."

"It's your client's brother, isn't it?" A flashback of Isaiah and Taylor's interaction in the courtroom comes to Dulaney's mind.

"Yup!"

"You didn't?" Dulaney remembers calling Taylor in Asia to share her first time.

"I did." Taylor follows the floating white clouds as she recalls the beautiful moment she shared with Isaiah.

"How was it?" Dulaney nudges her arm, waking her from the daydream.

"It was magnificent." Taylor glows as she mesmerizes the way Isaiah held her, touched her, caressed her, and kissed her. He explored every inch of her body.

"Wow! That good, huh?" The two friends exchanged laughs and prepared to depart the vineyard.

The train ride from Santa Barbara to Los Angeles is as exquisite as the trip up. Fatigue is upon Dulaney and Taylor after a day of elegant wines, fabulous food, beautiful views of the Pacific Ocean, and renewed friendship. On the short ride to the hotel, Delaney informs Taylor of her early departure. "I want to get back to Atlanta at a reasonable hour. My body needs to adjust to the time difference." The girls trade goodbyes at the 25th-floor elevator.

"Shall I help you pack?" Taylor asks Delaney.

"I'm good, Tay. I had fun today." Dulaney hugs Taylor, who stands in the hallway until Delaney reaches her door.

"Goodnight." They wave to each other, and Taylor makes a few short steps to her suite door, looking over her shoulder one last time before she enters.

The sunlight sifting through the partially closed drapes stirs Taylor. She checks for the time on the nightstand, only to be reminded she never put the docking station back. She drags herself out of bed and wobbles to the small sofa to retrieve her phone from her backpack. After scrolling through the missed calls and texts, ensuring none were from the court, she finally checks the time—9:44 a.m. Geez, breakfast is over.

Taylor moseys to the bathroom, showers, and dresses. A lovely brunch is fitting before she goes to the office. But first, she responds to Isaiah's calls and texts. *Hey, you. Got a min?* Isaiah calls her within seconds. "Hey, Counselor. I called you all day yesterday."

"Hi. Delaney and I went to the vineyard in Santa Barbara; the reception wasn't good."

Taylor invites Isaiah to brunch; he delightedly accepts.

They agree on rooftop dining at a nearby spot a short walk from the hotel. Taylor arrives before Isaiah and relishes in the impressive outdoor dining space. She orders Sangria while she awaits his arrival and absorbs the fresh air from atop. After he arrives, they order—French toast for Taylor and steak frites for Isaiah. They engage in conversation until their food comes—avoiding the elephant in the room. The ambiance is pleasing. Taylor loses track of time. It's almost 3:00 p.m. Isaiah notices her fidgeting at her watch, so he suggests they order tea and shifts to the lounge chairs. Taylor agrees, realizing she won't get any work done today. They move to an intimate setting where tea is served. Isaiah approaches the subject. "Taylor, I need to ask you something."

Taylor's muscles tighten. She foresees Isaiah's question. "Yes?"

Isaiah leans in, "A few weeks back when we—," his voice cracks. "When we made love, was it your first time?" Taylor dreads this conversation but knows it's unavoidable.

"Isaiah, I am sorry I didn't tell you. I lost myself in a beautiful moment, and I—," her voice quivers. The Counselor is lost for words and lowers her head, breaking eye contact with Isaiah. He is disoriented. Boyd gleaned this from a conversation, yet he didn't discern it despite his participation. He lifts Taylor's head and speaks affectionately. "I am honored you entrusted me with your most precious jewel," fondly kissing the back of her hand. Although he lets it down, he doesn't let it go. The lovebirds enjoy the afternoon music on the rooftop.

When Taylor returns to the hotel, she checks her calendar and email. Her phone buzzes at the same time her email dings. The verdict is in, and court resumes at 9:00 a.m. on Monday.

"All rise." The bailiff calls the court to order. "Court's now in session." Members of the courtroom stand, and the judge takes his seat on the bench as he taps his gavel. "Please be seated," he instructs. Studying the jury over the tip of his glasses, "Madam Foreperson, has the jury reached a verdict?"

The foreperson glares into the courtroom and to the defendant's table, "We have, Your Honor."

Judge Crane confirms, "You have signed and dated the verdict forms indicating the jury's verdict?"

"Yes, Your Honor," Madam Foreperson corroborates.

"Please pass the envelope to the deputy." While the deputy delivers the envelope to Judge Crane, he addresses the jury. "Thank you, ladies and gentlemen of the jury. I ask that you listen carefully. After the clerk reads the verdict, she will ask for your confirmation."

Directing the defendant, "Mr. Boyd Myers, will you please stand and face the jury." Boyd and Taylor stand, as instructed. She saw Boyd's tremble and prays he is not found guilty.

"Ms. Day, will you?" The judge concludes his instructions, and Ms. Day reads the verdict.

"Superior Court of California, County of Los Angeles. In the matter of People of the State of California vs. Boyd Myers, case number [01-898989]. We, the jury, in the above-entitled action, find the Defendant, Boyd Myers, not guilty ..."

Boyd's knees buckle. There are outward gasps from the court.

"Order, order," Judge Crane raps his gavel. "I will clear the courtroom with another outburst."

Hansen steadies Boyd and Ms. Day read on.

"...of the crime of attempted murder in violation of penal code section 187, a felony, upon Detective Franklin, a human being, as charged in the Information. Signed this 14th day of November 2019. Ladies and gentlemen of the jury, is this your verdict? So say you one, so say you all."

"Yes," and more gasps disrupt throughout the courtroom.

"Quiet in the courtroom," the judge warns again.

Boyd never doubted his innocence but to hear the twelve strangers who held his fate realized it too, overwhelmed him. He stumbles into his chair, and Taylor sees he is overcome with relief.

Judge Crane then instructs the clerk. "Ms. Day, will you please poll the jurors?"

The clerk begins, "Juror No. 1, is this your verdict?"

Juror No. 1 replies with a sheer "Yes," holding the listless face each of the twelve wore the entire trial. Ms. Day polls each juror, receiving a yes from all twelve. When she finishes, the judge gives further instruction, and the courtroom quiets.

"All right. Ms. Day, please record the verdict as read. Thank you, ladies and gentlemen of the jury, for your service. The court is indebted to you for the time, patience, and exertion you gave during this trial." The judge makes his final remarks and dismisses the jury. "I now excuse you from further service in this case."

Judge Crane faces the defendant's table and tells Boyd, "Mr. Boyd Myers, you are acquitted of the charge of attempted murder; you are free to go." The judge's intuition told him Boyd was innocent. It is something about Boyd's demeanor that is wholesome, not rehearsed.

Boyd is subjugated with a myriad of emotions. He can't feel his legs; he doesn't think he can stand. "Thank you, Your Honor." His sigh of relief is palpable. All he wants is to walk outside. He recalls wondering earlier if it was his last walk as a free man on downtown streets. He has a renewed appreciation right now.

Judge Crane sounds his gavel against the bench one last time.

Boyd sits motionless. Taylor places her hand on his shoulder while he processes he is free to go. When Isaiah approaches, she steps aside, giving him space to console his brother. All the emotions Boyd repressed rushes to the forefront when Isaiah hugs him. He collapses in Isaiah's arms, and the brothers lock arms until Boyd composes himself.

As the brothers embrace, Hansen engulfs Taylor in a bear hug, "You did it, Counselor!" Pure excitement emits from him.

"Hansen, I can't breathe." When Hansen releases his hug, Taylor turns to Boyd to explain post-trial procedures.

Although he regained his composure, Boyd couldn't think of post-trial stuff. "Do you mind if this part waits?" Taylor consents. "We'll schedule a time next week to talk."

Boyd is grateful for Taylor and Hansen's work. Seeing her in action in the courtroom reveals her commitment to defending her client. "Thank you very much. I am sorry I doubted you." He shakes Hansen's hand with gratitude.

"Join your folks. We'll talk later," Taylor urges Boyd. She rests her elbow on Hansen's shoulder and respires. "Let's get a drink."

On the steps of the courthouse is the media frenzy Boyd slithered through when he arrived. This time, he stands, shoulders squared, and head held high, as Taylor responds to the reporters. "Our legal team proved my client's innocence. The jury did their job, and justice was served."

One of the reporters asks Boyd for a statement. "This was the worst nightmare of my life. I am grateful to my lawyers and the jury for believing in my innocence."

Taylor gives final words to the media before leaving the courthouse. "My client showed dignity and great moral strength. He should be proud of the justice system, as should you. Thank you."

After a glass of Pinot Noir and a beer, Taylor and Hansen return to the office. When they enter the reception area,

Cathy beams with excitement. "Congratulations, you two!" In unison, "thank you."

Taylor sits at her desk, scrolling through her playlist. She tunes to one of her favorite gospel songs and dances in her chair to the dynamic beats; the lyrics are appropriate for the occasion.

As she swirls around, Mr. Daniels and the Mayor stand before her. Embarrassed, she gestures to the chairs, "Gentlemen, please have a seat," removing her earbuds.

"I suppose you deserve a victory dance," the Mayor assumes as he greets Taylor. "I understand you did a superb job in the courtroom, and I'm not the least bit surprised." The Mayor trusts Taylor's abilities as a trial lawyer; he often recommends her to friends, clients, and family.

"Glory to God and thank you." Taylor raises her hands in prayer position toward the Mayor, who chuckles before he recommences. "I bet that's what you were doing when we walked in, praising God?" He knew Taylor since she was yay high and shared in her family's faith in God.

Unassumingly, "Yes."

She and the Mayor's relationship is long-standing. He and her father were long-time friends; they met in law school. They practiced law together for a short time many years ago. The Mayor was instrumental in Taylor going to law school, keeping his promise to her father—his friend—to look out for her. She even clerked for him her first year.

The Mayor is well acquainted with Taylor's struggle of losing her father. She was a young girl when her dad passed. He believes the loss of her father led her closer to God. "Your faith will guide you over, young lady. Don't ever waiver." He gives her the fatherly wink as he does when he offers her advice.

She accepts the Mayor's wisdom. "I won't." Taylor scans her vibrating phone before shifting the conversation. "We must defend post-trial motions. I'll explain to Boyd. He wanted a moment to celebrate his victory, so I told him we could talk later."

Confused, the Mayor peers questioningly above the rim of his eyeglasses to get a clearer perspective. "Celebrate?"

"Yes. Boyd asked for a moment. I assumed it is to celebrate." The Mayor's bewilderment puzzles Taylor.

"Sweetheart, he's doing what you were in here doing—praising God." Taylor is aware of the Mayor's faith, but she isn't privy to Boyd's belief system. The topic hasn't surfaced between her and Isaiah, but she is glad to hear. "Oh!" Taylor is surprised.

"Family and faith, remember." The Mayor knows Taylor's dad lived by that motto. As a growing girl, she recited it more times than not. Her dad's presence envelops her when she echoes it. Apparently, the Mayor instilled the same motto in his family.

"I am well pleased; your father would be too. I head back to Atlanta tonight." The Mayor mimics Taylor's reverence by raising his hand in a prayer position. "And, take it easy on Isaiah." Not waiting for her reaction regarding his nephew, he persists. "Keep me updated on the post-trial motions. And let me know if you need anything." Taylor disregards the Mayor's sly comment about Isaiah and leverages the moment to discuss her need, though it is unrelated to the case.

"Speaking of needs, there is one thing." Taylor reaches for her attaché and retrieves the proposal requesting a donation for her Center. "The kids at the Center would love it if your office donates a computer," she hands the Mayor the manila envelope. Mr. Daniels was quiet the entire time, but now boasts of his generous donation. "Our firm donated ten." He looks to Taylor as if to say, let him match our donation.

Mayor Sellect waves off Mr. Daniels and accepts the envelope from Taylor. "I will deliver this request to our office, and I will personally donate two computers. You are doing a wonderful job with those kids." Taylor acknowledges the authenticity in the Mayor's commendation.

"Dinner is on me when you return home, young lady."

"I look forward to dinner, thank you."

"If my nephew has his way, I have a feeling you'll have plenty of dinners with me."

A strange sound disrupts their conversation. The Mayor gets his phone from inside his pocket. "My nephew," he signifies and answers. After a brief talk, he looks to Taylor and says, "I am instructed to bring you with me to Nick and Stef's for 5:45 p.m." He clinches the chance to tease Taylor about having dinners with him, emphasizing the plural dinners. "Told you..."

Making an assumption, "I presume your nephew directed you?" She vowed to talk to Isaiah after the verdict, but she isn't in the mood. She wants only to unwind with a movie and martini.

"That is correct."

"Thank you, but I promised Hansen dinner." Taylor lied.

The Mayor is dubious. Isaiah warned him she might give that excuse. "Hansen can join us."

Just then, Hansen enters Taylor's office. "Join whom? For what?" he asks, surveying the room. He looks from Taylor to Mr. Daniels to Mayor Sellect, awaiting someone to fill him in.

"Mayor Sellect wants us to join his family for dinner, but I told him you and I have plans." Taylor inconspicuously tries to coax Hansen.

"Oh, we do?"

Hansen's inability to fall in line with Taylor is the confirmation the Mayor needs. Without further discussion, he announces, "the car picks us up at 5:15 p.m. See you out front," and he exits her office. Mr. Daniels follows. When he approaches the doorway, he bolsters, "They have great martinis," and disappears down the corridor.

Hansen apologetically asks Taylor, "I blew that; didn't I?"

"Yup!" Taylor drops her face inside the palms of her hands.

Hansen explores Taylor's angst. "What's your trepidation with dinner?"

Taylor hunches her shoulders, implying, I don't know. They sit in silence for a few minutes before Taylor explains she is tired and wants to be alone. They chat about the next steps in the case before agreeing the discussion can wait until tomorrow.

At 5:10 p.m. Taylor pokes her head in Hansen's office to find it empty. It is bizarre he'd go downstairs without her. But she turns on the heel of her shoe and goes to the elevator, waving goodnight to Cathy. Hansen is nowhere in sight when she reaches the sidewalk; he pulled one on her!

The ride to the restaurant is pleasant. When they arrive at the South Hope Street restaurant, the maître d' escorts them to the rooftop. It is a lovely evening for rooftop dining, and the ambiance is astounding.

Isaiah arranged a dinner party with Boyd's close friends to celebrate his victory. When they reach the table, "Let's give a round of applause to the lady who made it happen."

Cheers resound from the table, with someone chanting, "Speech."

Taylor was not expecting this. She looks to the Mayor and then to Boyd, who walks up and hands her a drink. "We ordered a Cosmo with Goose for you. Here's a scotch on the rocks for you, Uncle."

Lifting her glass, she bids, "To Boyd." The guests cheer, and she sips her martini, which is mixed to perfection.

Sliding a chair from under the table, Isaiah motions for Taylor to have a seat. The Mayor and Isaiah take seats on each side of her.

"Counselor, what's next for you? Do you leave for Atlanta soon?" He dreads the answer.

His questions come as she drinks from her martini. Placing the glass onto the table, "Not just yet. There's post-trial work." Astonishingly, she's been in Los Angeles eight weeks.

Her answer delights Isaiah. He has time to grow their relationship with her nearby. "Good," he grins. "That means I get to grace you with my presence longer."

"Does it?" She and Isaiah have fun and genuinely appreciate each other's charisma. Her hiatus from the last weeks put space between them, but they desire to nurture their budding relationship.

He brush-offs Taylor's shade and embraces her smart remark. "Absolutely; starting this weekend. Go to Tahoe with me?" Isaiah looks to his Uncle, who seemingly enjoys the banter between him and Taylor, for support. "You deserve a break before you dive into your post-trial work." Isaiah pleads, again looking to his Uncle, hoping he chimes in.

The Mayor laughs inwardly at his nephew's begging, and without success, he might add. "Tahoe is a nice place to rest or have fun," the Mayor finally reinforces his nephew's imploration. Isaiah's expression to his Uncle infers; it's about time.

"We'll see." The waiter rescues Taylor, arriving with their dinner. Besides, before she plans anything, she needs details from Coltrane on the fundraiser for her youth center. Isaiah accepts her maybe; it isn't a flat-out no, and that he can work it.

Boyd's celebration makes for a pleasant evening. She wishes Hansen joined them. As the victory dinner comes to an end, Taylor opts for a cab ride to the hotel, and Isaiah drives his Uncle to LAX.

Walking out of her shoes as she enters her hotel suite and shedding her clothing by the time she reaches the bathroom, Taylor steps into the shower. Sleep is upon her.

Isaiah's request to visit Tahoe remains top of her mind while she prepares for bed. Never visiting Tahoe, she heard beautiful testimonies about its beaches and ski resorts. She plays the weekend in her brain, but her thoughts drift to her youth center's fundraiser. Her first call when she arrives at the office in the morning is to Coltrane to discuss details. For now, it's lights out.

"Good morning, Counselor," Taylor hears entering the elevator. It's crowded. She isn't sure it's meant for her until she sees Hansen out of the corner of her eye. When they reach their floor, Taylor waits for Hansen before proceeding to their office. Cathy whispers, pointing to the conference room, "Something has Mr. Daniels on edge. He wants to see you." Taylor and Hansen look between Cathy and each other puzzled before Hansen blurts out, "For what?"

"I don't know." Taylor and Hansen go to the conference room and stand quietly in the doorway while Mr. Daniels yells into the speakerphone. After he ends the call, they step into the room. Hansen asks, "Everything okay?"

Mr. Daniels hurls, "Plan to join me in the Atlanta office on Wednesday?" He gathers his files and storms out. Taylor and Hansen look at each other, confounded.

Taylor ruminates on what has Mr. Daniels furious and the need for travel to Atlanta. The trip to Atlanta creates an opportunity to see her youth and get details from Coltrane about the fundraiser. She dreads bringing up the bombshell Delaney dropped on her, but that's also a conversation she intends to have with Coltrane. After a few minutes of introspection, Taylor retreats to her office.

Her first order of business is her youth center. She calls the landline, and Chantell answers in an upbeat tone, "Good morning. How may I assist you?" Taylor delights at the commitment Chantell makes to the Center and the pleasantries she extends to everyone. "Hi, Chaney!" Taylor nicknamed her the first day she walked into the Center.

Chantell's excitement to hear Taylor's voice is vibrant. "Ms. Alexander! We miss you!" Taylor's eyes well with water; she misses them too. She often wonders if they know the joy they bestow upon her. "I miss you too! How are you?" Memories of the youth flicker through her mind, rendering her overawed. Chantell eagerly shares her recent happenings with Taylor before she asks about the fundraiser.

Coltrane is near Chantell's desk and believes he heard her say Taylor's name. He wonders why she didn't call his cell but isn't positive it is, in fact, Taylor on the phone. Moving closer to Chantell's desk, she announces, "It's Ms. Alexander." Chantell gave Taylor insights into the fundraiser plans, which prepared her for the discussion with Coltrane. Chantell hands the receiver to Coltrane. "What's up, Tay?"

She treads carefully because she cannot reveal Delaney leaked his secret. "It's all about you. How's it going?" She and Coltrane discuss the fundraiser and donations and exchange a few pleasantries. "I will be in Atlanta on Wednesday. I don't have a full schedule, but I will definitely come by to see my children." Coltrane laughs at her genuineness when she refers to the youth as her children. "And, I amassed twelve computers."

Coltrane is tickled and perplexed. Since establishing the Center, she asked no one to donate computers. Yet, in a few weeks, she collects twelve. "I see! Ten arrived this morning. We may reach our goal, Tay!"

"Thank you, Knucklehead, for motivating me to upgrade the computers." Taylor wraps up the call; careful not to allude to the wife and children Coltrane hides from her. "I have to run, but I'll see you on Wednesday."

Coltrane obliges, "We can review the fundraiser details then."

Wednesday's face-to-face is her real test. The trial distracted her, leaving no time to think about it. But she hurts. Her lifelong friend withheld such information from her. Why?

An incoming call from Isaiah intrudes on Taylor's thoughts. She'll call him back after she finds out why Mr. Daniel's is in a knot. She responds with an automated message that reads; please allow me to return your call at a more suitable time. Soon after, she's down the hall to Mr. Daniel's office, hoping he settled down from his call earlier. Surprisingly, he is not in his office.

In her office, Taylor pulls out files from her attaché to review, but her mind floats to Isaiah's request to join him in Tahoe. Is Isaiah winning her over? "Focus, Taylor," she mumbles to herself and opens the file folder. In her review, she stumbles upon something she missed beforehand. It reminds her to follow up with Cathy on her research on the Myers brothers. She dials 0 for the reception, "Cathy, did your research uncover warfare between Isaiah and Boyd?"

"No, but I'll send the information to you on the next mail run." Cathy's tone causes Taylor to raise her eyebrows. "Okay. Thank you." And Taylor continues to review the documents.

Sometime later, she receives a text message from Isaiah inviting her to lunch. She agrees to a late lunch and continues working until Cathy calls to remind her she has a lunch appointment. "Oh, did I overlook something on my schedule?" Cathy reassures her she is neither double-booked nor did she overlook an appointment. Mr. Isaiah Myers asked her to remind Taylor of their lunch. She jokes with Cathy, "Did he ask you to christen the firstborn too?" She shocks herself. Cathy laughs with Taylor as they end the call so Taylor can meet Isaiah for lunch.

Taylor met Isaiah at the market, where they order wood-fired pizzas and salads. They opt for a table on the outdoor patio because the weather is pleasant. The sun glistens off Taylor's caramel skin, and Isaiah admires her as she picks at her salad. He wonders if she held a person's past against him. He didn't intend to ask, but the words released from his thought. "Would you hold a bad decision in someone's past against them?" Taylor's radar is on full alert. Isaiah's question triggers the moment the Mayor said the brothers forgave each other. Containing her eagerness to hear of this questionable judgment, she raises her head from her salad plate, "Depends on the bad decision." They hold each other's stare momentarily before Isaiah breaks it and bites into his pizza.

After he swallows, he probes further. "What is your deal-breaker in a relationship?" Taylor once believed cheating was her deal-breaker. A few years ago, she discovered she might explore the underlying reason for cheating. That's not to say she would stay, but she is willing to listen. For her, that is growth. "Lying. And yes, a lie by omission qualifies."

He considers Taylor's stance. Is it tied to a prior experience? "Interesting. Why lying?" Isaiah sits back in his chair, arms folded, while Taylor finishes the last bite of salad.

"Lying indicates a different—sometimes bigger issue. When you trust yourself to be vulnerable, there's no need to lie." Taylor examines Isaiah for his reaction. He stares vacantly, as if he is in a battle with himself.

She commits this moment to memory. "What about you? What yours?"

Isaiah leans forward and smiles at Taylor. "How about I share with you over a glass of wine this evening? I need to get back for a meeting."

"Nice way to avoid the question."

"Is that what you think?" Isaiah is impressed with her comeback. He does need to think about his. It's not as rudimentary to him.

"Is that what it is?"

She just said lying is her deal-breaker, so that's out of the question. He has a meeting, although he can spare more time. "I promise to confess the glory details over a glass of wine. What time will you end your day?"

"I can't go tonight. I have to pack." Isaiah is startled. Didn't she say she has post-trial stuff to handle? "Pack?" His confusion is visible.

The moment is precious. Taylor torments, "Yes. I am heading to Atlanta tomorrow."

Frantic, Isaiah inquires. "I thought you have post-trial something or another?" He couldn't remember exactly. "Were you going to tell me you're leaving tomorrow?" Isaiah's disappointment manifests more than the confusion on his face. Taylor comes clean.

"I am not leaving. Mr. Daniels requested I accompany him to the Atlanta office tomorrow. I will stay a few days to check on the Center." Taylor observes the creases in Isaiah's forehead unfold, and the tension in his body relaxes. He slides his chair from the table, stands, and reaches for her hand. She joins her hand with his as she stands, and he pulls her to him. Wrapping his arms around her, "Don't tease like that." He plants a kiss on her forehead, and they depart to their respective offices.

Taylor checks again for Mr. Daniels in his office. He sits at the round table, sifting through documents. Tapping on the door, "Got a minute?" He motions for her to join him. Taylor pulls out the chair, and Mr. Daniels reaches a single piece of paper to her. "What's this?" Taylor asks as she reads. What in the world? How can this be? "This was not in discovery."

Pointing around his office without lifting his head, "This shall not leave these four walls."

"Is this why we're going to Atlanta tomorrow?"

"Yes." Mr. Daniels shakes his head.

"May I have a copy?"

"It's on your desk. The partners want to get ahead of this. Tomorrow's a strategy meeting. Come prepared." With that, he stands and gathers the documents. Taylor follows suit. As she reaches the doorway, she asks, "Do you believe the Mayor is in on this?"

Mr. Daniels looks squarely at Taylor, scratching his head. "I hope he isn't."

The results of Cathy's investigation of the Myers brothers and the binder, presumably with copies of the documents Mr. Daniels shared, await Taylor when she returns to her office. She places the envelope with Cathy's results in her attaché and tucks the binder under her arm. She will work for the rest of the day from her hotel.

Two thoughts consume Taylor on her walk to the hotel; 1) Coltrane's secret and 2) Mayor Sellect's alleged involvement in Detective Franklin's shooting.

Taylor and Mr. Daniels reach the mid-town Atlanta building shortly before 2:00 p.m. EST. The conference room is filled with sandwiches, pasta, salad, and fruit. "Looks like we'll be here a while." Mr. Daniels doesn't hear her. She texts Delaney, letting her know she is home for a few days. Excited to see her rugrats (as Dulaney called them), she quickly calls the Center to let Chantell know she arrived. By now, folks are filing into the conference room. While familiar with all the lawyers, there's one gentleman she doesn't know.

After hours of discussion, accusations, and opinions, the group of lawyers agrees to resume at 11:00 a.m. tomorrow. Taylor is surprised by the late start, but pleased. It allows her time to stop by the Center. As they wrap up, Mr. Daniels invites her to dinner.

"Mind if I have a rain check? I'd like to go home." Mr. Daniels accepts Taylor's renunciation, and she's off to reacquaint herself with her home. But her first stop is the Robert Taylor Alexander Youth Development Center.

It's a short ride to downtown, and when the driver pulls up, Taylor beams. She hops out of the SUV, thanks the driver, and heads to the door. Fumbling for her keys, Coltrane startles her when he opens the door from inside. "You're here late!" Taylor steps in.

"Is that how you greet your friend who babysat for two months? Come on here and hug me!" Coltrane wraps his arm around Taylor's neck. All the emotions she faced about his secret life gusts to the forefront.

Her unusual demeanor concerns Coltrane. "You okay? What's wrong?"

Taylor is quick on her feet and usually doesn't filter. But she is stock-still.

"Taylor, what's wrong?" Coltrane shakes her.

"Stop it!" Taylor isn't prepared for this conversation. She did not realize the depth of her feelings until now. Betrayed by one of the few persons she calls friend, family. "You tell me. You're the one keeping secrets." Her words flow with venom.

Coltrane is clueless. "What are you talking about?"

"Oh, play stupid!" Taylor walks to Chantell's desk, where she places her attaché. Coltrane closes the door and follows. "What the hell are you talking about, Tay?"

Taylor faces him straightaway. She did not intend to have this conversation tonight. But she is face-to-face with the person who is supposed to be one of her best friends, and her emotions are uncontrolled. "Why is it I have to find out in the rumor mill you have a wife and twin girls?"

Coltrane can dig a hole in the very spot he stands and bury himself. Why did Delaney tell Taylor?

"You have nothing to say?"

Coltrane watches Taylor's mouth move, but he doesn't hear a word she says. His mind trapped him, fretting over what caused Dulaney to share this information. "Taylor, you don't know the whole story." Taylor continually attacks him.

"You are right about that! I don't know any part of the story. What I know is, the person I call friend—family—lied to me." Her condescension turns to a whimper. The hurt is discernible in her tone and her body language. Coltrane is taken aback by the rare display of Taylor's vulnerability. He steps toward her; she steps back, out of his reach. "You can't even deny it!" She never thought Delaney didn't tell the truth, though she hoped it wasn't true.

"Taylor... " Again, he steps closer to her. "...Let me explain." Coltrane isn't sure he wants to explain, but Taylor's agony is unbearable.

"Why explain today? You didn't divulge before." Taylor storms into her office and closes the door. She is grateful to Coltrane. He kept her Center operational for the past months. But right now, she can't look at him. Through the madness with Delaney, she remained loyal, never taking sides. They played her like a game of table tennis, and it does not make her feel good. Coltrane realizes there is no getting through to Taylor. He waits for her to come out of her office. When she doesn't, he gives her space. He texts Delaney—*you shouldn't have told her.*

Once Taylor settled down, she noticed the blueprint Coltrane designed for the fundraiser on her desk. She also notes—and likes—the rearrangement of her office. She thoroughly reviews the plans. After evaluating them, she peeks through the doorway, hoping Coltrane left. He is nowhere in sight. She applauds his adjustments. He moved the computer area away from gaming, but the reading area remains tucked in the back. Before Taylor leaves, she writes a message in plain sight for Coltrane. It reads, I like the enhancements, and I am forever grateful to you for sacrificing your agency to keep mine functional. I also hurt to my core you didn't share your children with me. Talk later, Tay.

Taylor is mentally and physically exhausted by the time she gets home. A familiar aroma meets her when the elevator opens to her unit. Thank God Mr. Hunt prepared dinner. Taylor ate the home-cooked grilled steak and asparagus. She refills her glass of Malbec and wanders to the window as Isaiah occupies her thoughts. It would be nice for him to wrap his arms around me tonight.

After a short while, she pulls out the case file the lawyers discussed, argued over, made accusations, and formed opinions about earlier today. She has a notion she cannot shake, but she needs to substantiate it. Therefore, she searches the file like it's a needle in a haystack, retreating to bed at midnight, not revealing anything concrete.

Before turning the lamp off, she checks her phone. She missed calls from Isaiah and Delaney and a text from Coltrane that read; *I am sorry*. Assuming he goes to the center in the morning, he'll see her note. She will call Delaney and Isaiah tomorrow.

CHAPTER 7

The Truth

The group of lawyers recommences with deliberations about the photograph, revealing unfounded evidence in Boyd's attempted murder case. Notably, Mr. Daniels isn't in the room. Taylor considers his whereabouts. Did he visit the mayor? He was adamant about keeping the picture discreet. Does the picture surprise him? Or is he surprised the image is leaked? She listens and weighs all opinions in the room until one of the lawyers challenges her. "Did you know about this?" She didn't recognize him, and it slipped her mind to ask who is he.

"How dare you!"

"We all know you're like a daughter to the mayor. You'd do anything to please him."

"Need I remind you—all of you—I earned my law degree, just like the rest of you? And I won't sacrifice it, or my father's name, for the mayor or anyone else? You can go to hell, or wherever you come from!"

Mr. Daniels enters the room in time to hear the end of the accusation. He does not know Taylor as well as the mayor, but he knew her father. He was no stranger to integrity. "Settle down, settle down. Our job is to verify the legitimacy of the image. Accusations won't get us anywhere. Like it or not, Ms. Alexander leads this team."

Taylor appreciates Mr. Daniels, but she can hold her own with the suits in the room. "Thank you, Mr. Daniels. Now, does anyone know where the picture originated? Are there leads on the photographer?" The lawyers resolve and collaborate to gather facts around the photo. It's no coincidence it appeared one day after Boyd was acquitted of attempted murder.

"Ms. Alexander, an anonymous caller insists he speaks only to you." The receptionist holds for direction. The attorneys exchange expressions and look at Taylor for her reaction.

"Put him through." They wait anxiously for the receptionist to transfer the call. "Not a sound from anyone."

Despite expecting the call transfer, the phone startled everyone when it rang. "Taylor Alexander, may I help you?"

"You can start by taking me off of speaker," the caller demands. Taylor motions for Mr. Daniels to pick up the side phone as she handles the primary receiver. "The speakerphone is turned off."

"Meet me at your center at 3:00 p.m. if you want information about the photo." Holy shit! The caller researched her.

"No dice. Not around my kids." Taylor makes a mental note to secure her center and Mr. Hunt's home. She doesn't use security habitually, but the conglomerate dedicates a team of former CIA agents to her. Mr. Hunt insinuated a time or two before her dad sends orders from heaven. It leads her to believe security covers her inconspicuously.

"Centennial Park by the water splash." One of the lawyers holds up a note that reads *too many civilians*.

"Your center, or as you said, no dice. 3 o'clock," the caller hangs up.

"You can't do this," Mr. Daniels barks. The others observe inquisitorially.

"Like hell I can," Taylor snarls back and shares the details of the call. Immediately after that, she dials the conglomerate to arrange a security detail. She needs a plan to clear the center without alarming Coltrane or the kids, and quickly.

"Hey, Joe. I need the team but keep it quiet." Taylor provides particulars to Joe while the lawyers observe. After, she convinces Coltrane to bring the kids to the water splash at Centennial Park.

"What if this fool is dangerous? I can't take the risk, Taylor." Mr. Daniels pleads with her.

"I'll go with you," her accuser from earlier chimes in.

"Me too," another says. Mr. Daniels drops into a chair, defeated.

Taylor leans to him. "You want the truth, don't you? This may lead us to it. Trust us. There are well-trained agents to protect us." Her plan is inconceivable, foolish, and dangerous, but they won't let her go alone.

Joe coordinates the security. He places two guys on the perimeter, a marksman on the roof across the street, and hides two guys inside the center. He replaces Taylor's driver with himself. All set.

The SUV pulls to the entrance of the center, and the volunteers climb out of the back. One of them opens Taylor's door and helps her out. Joe remains in the driver's seat. Taylor and the volunteer lawyers wait for the caller for two hours. He does not show. Mr. Daniels is on pins and needles when they return to the office. His relief is discernible as Taylor explains the caller did not show. The ringing phone stops her, and she presses the speaker button. "You should have come alone," the caller hangs up. Realizing the caller unknowingly watched them at the youth center sent chills through Taylor's vein.

She closes her center on Friday out of caution and tells Coltrane it's because of an electrical issue. Assigning tasks to the team of lawyers, "Who wants to review the file analytically, decipher all leads? We need to find the photographer, anyone?" She points to the lawyer who accused her earlier, "You and I are interrogators; be prepared. Who wants to go undercover at my center, in case the caller shows?" All assignments are planned for each lawyer to work in their area of specialty. She will check in Monday morning before going back to Los Angeles.

Mr. Daniels, however, returns to Los Angeles while she spends the weekend at home. It is good to be home, even if only for a few days. Besides, Isaiah arrives mid-morning on Friday.

After a full week of work, the four-hour flight, and the chaos of the anonymous caller Taylor is spent. She is rarely fatigued. But this morning, she lies in bed longer, drawn-out only by the smell of Mr. Hunt's breakfast. She meanders across the beautifully polished floor without slippers and stares out the window, nibbling on a piece of bacon.

"Good morning, young lady." Mr. Hunt's voice is music to her ears. It reminds her she is home. It's been weeks since she heard his good morning. Taylor turns away from the view of the cityscape to her loyal wingman—Mr. Hunt is much more than her help. He stands before her, ready to serve breakfast.

"Those words ring with such melody. I miss you!" Taylor hugs Mr. Hunt and takes her seat at the counter.

"Case stressing you?" He pours a mimosa, placing it in front of her.

"Not until this week. Key evidence surfaced after the trial. It's not good for my client."

"You always figure it out! Set it aside for a while."

"I will. Don't be alarmed by the detail covering you." Mr. Hunt doesn't like the security detail any more than she does.

"They showed up last night. Anything to do with this evidence you mentioned?" Mr. Hunt has been in the family long enough to know the ins and outs of cases. He traveled this journey with her father. "You watch out for yourself. I am good."

"I'm fine." Taylor finishes the pancakes, bacon, and mimosa. She retreats to the coziness of her bed until Isaiah arrives.

It is the perfect day to be on the water. White puffy clouds are crafted into works of art in the clear blue sky. A breeze blows beautifully off the water and sunshine beams on the lake. The docility of the wind raggers the water enough to create waves but not make the tides fuss. Mother Nature's elements align to perfection, but neither Isaiah nor Taylor sailed without a licensed captain. Today, their skills are tested.

After a few glitches, Isaiah figures out the headsail, and they are on their way to relax on the water under the sun. Taylor removes her sundress to reveal the black one-piece with a diagonal cutout across the navel, causing Isaiah, who is finishing with the mainsail, to lose focus. She is beautiful. The sun's rays radiate off her skin. Her curly hair floats past her shoulders, down her back. The wind blows a strain across her face, and Isaiah's eyes dip to take in her beauty. As she applies sunscreen to her legs, Isaiah makes it his point to offer aid. "Let me help you," he says and eases the container from her hand. The simple task of applying sunscreen to her back makes him giddy.

Taylor utters not a single word, but her body stiffens as he caresses her back. Thoughts of the evening they spent together that almost changed their budding relationship's trajectory flashed into their minds. Isaiah slows the circular motions he makes across her back and asks with compassion, "You okay?" Taylor says nothing as she looks at the sun's reflection off the water. If she is honest with herself, she enjoys his touch—it is soothing in a way she cannot articulate. Captivated by her thoughts, she does not realize Isaiah is finished until he places the container back into her hands. He returns to fighting with the sails while Taylor soaks in the sun, occasionally admiring the curves of her outstretched body. His mind wanders to the smoothness of her skin and how soft it felt against his body. The sensations of his body remind him to focus on the sails.

When Isaiah concludes his fight with the sails, he joins Taylor in the sun. He undressed to his trunks after he applied the sunscreen to her back. They lay hypnotized by the sounds of the water, softly touching hands and enjoying each other's presence. There's an unspoken language between them. After floating on the water for some time, Isaiah docks the boat in an alcove where they set up lunch on the sand. The surrounding trees provide shade while allowing them to absorb the sun. Isaiah explores every inch of her as Taylor spread the blanket. The way she moves put him in a trance, and it didn't help her swimsuit is accentuating her curves. Without realizing it, he says out loud, "Get it together, dude." Taylor stops and looks up at him, "Huh?" Isaiah recognizes his thought made its way into the atmosphere. Embarrassed, he lies, "I was humming the song." The Bluetooth remains connected on the boat, so the music plays. He fails to convince Taylor he was singing, but she didn't comprehend his murmuring, so she doesn't interrogate.

After laying out the spread from the basket she packed, she sits on the blanket across from Isaiah, who inspects her arrangement. First, he notices the Cabernet Sauvignon and two wine glasses followed by a charcuterie board covered with cured meats, cheeses, crackers, fruit, nuts, pita bread, and hummus. Next to the board are two small salads. Isaiah wonders when she prepared the spread between the late meetings and the time she spends at her center. She inspires him. Taylor is one of those girls who make things happen—business, personal, and social.

Taylor interrupted Isaiah's thoughts when she said, "You wanna bless the food?" It is clear to him she isn't asking because she is reaching out to join hands with him. He takes her hands into his—he loves touching her—and blesses the food. He doesn't want to let her hand go. "When did you do all this?"

"Like it?" She's tempted to let him believe she prepared their lunch. Her friend, who has a flourishing boards and platters business, arranged the basket. Not giving him a chance to answer, "It is catered from one of my friends."

It doesn't matter to him she didn't prepare the food. He loves her just for being. Wishing he had an Isley Brothers song to say what he feels, he buries his feelings under a smile.

They explore casual conversation and enjoy the items from the lunch basket. Isaiah has a moment of regret as his thoughts drift to elements of his past, wondering if they will ruin his budding relationship. He abandons his thoughts and embraces the possibilities with the lady who sits before him. When they are finished eating but still sipping on the Cabernet Sauvignon, Isaiah momentarily slips away to the boat.

He returns to the blanket, sitting closer to Taylor, and hands her a small blue box with a neatly tied white bow. "I thought you would love it." Taylor is amazed by the blue box and slowly pulls one end of the white bow to unravel it. Filled with joy, she thanks Isaiah. "It is beautiful; thank you." Taylor studies the pendant designed in the image of a red wine bottle. On the back is an engraved T. It is lovely. She hugs Isaiah to show her gratitude.

Not wanting to let her go—she belongs in his arms—he tenderly kisses her cheek. Feeling only a slight tenseness from Taylor's body, he takes a chance and kisses her cheek again, this time moving closer to her mouth. He delicately pulls her bottom lip, sensing her jittery, but she doesn't resist. Isaiah pulls back, but he's close enough to feel her breath. "Why are you apprehensive about me?"

The heat of embarrassment covers Taylor's face. She pulls from his embrace and turns onto her stomach, resting on both elbows, staring into the lake. The tide's rippling flow brings ease upon her. "Vulnerability is not my strong point." Her voice travels over the lake. As the words flow from her lips, she wonders to herself why. A key element of strength is to be vulnerable. She hears her father's voice ringing in her ear. They're meant to complement each other, her father once told her. For her, the two present conflict.

"You don't strike me as one who grapples with being vulnerable," Isaiah comes back without drawing closer to her. He is in the perfect position to observe every twitch and twinkle as she speaks.

Fixated on the flowing water and not turning to face Isaiah, Taylor opens up. It isn't her intent, but the words roll off her tongue with ease. "It wasn't always a struggle, but after my dad's passing..." She pauses at her realization she is opening up and consciously explores the emotions stirring within. This is her reckoning, and before this moment, she never processed the feelings that arise when vulnerability greets her. Usually, she quickly dismisses her feelings with a diversion. Today, she allows herself to experience emotion. Isaiah isn't sure what's happening but sits quietly, allowing space for her reflection.

When Taylor comes out of her experience, still staring over the lake, she shares. "Sorry! I've never embraced my personal reckoning." Isaiah places his hand on the small of her back for comfort as she resumes. "After my dad's passing, I stopped feeling. I told myself if I don't feel, I couldn't hurt." Taylor surprises herself because she never spoke those words. The truth is, she's not sure if she recognized and or acknowledged that before now. The only outward emotions Taylor embraces are for her youth at the center— they are pure joy.

Recognizing the tremble in her voice, Isaiah lay next to her, also supported by his elbows. "That was brave of you. Thank you for trusting me enough to share." He isn't sure if Taylor trusted him as much as it was her recognizing her struggle. Either way, he is glad to be the one with whom she shares. Placing his finger under her chin, slightly turning her head to face him, "You are safe with me." And without waiting for a response, he consumes her full mouth, exploring the insides of her jawlines from east to west. Their tongues tangled, and the pleasure they feel is palpable. Not breaking the kiss, Isaiah pulls Taylor into his body and lies back onto the blanket where they enjoyed lunch, pushing aside remnants of the basket. The warmth of her mouth sets a blazing fire throughout his body. It feels damn good, and he hopes every moment he spends with her feels this way. Breaking the passion brewing between them, Isaiah whispers, "I can resist a lot of things; temptation isn't one of them."

Defying the sexual tension and temptation pervading their space, the two opt to explore the abandoned land before picking up the anchor. As they navigate the looming trees and undefined rubbish of the land, Isaiah tells Taylor of his plans to own a vineyard. It reminds her of the last memory she shared with her dad. Isaiah is thrilled to share his vision and welcomed her thoughts. She is smart with a sharp wit and makes him laugh; because her jokes are corny.

When they make it back to the boat, Isaiah pulls the anchor out of the water while Taylor changes. Thank God for packing a second swimsuit. She snagged her cover-up on a tree.

Enjoying the lake, she lounges on the front of the boat while Isaiah pushes buttons on a panel. The soft breeze blows as the sun scorches her skin. Isaiah peeks at her from behind the sunshades he wears. She catches him but looks away while his eyes continue to travel the length of her body.

"Thank you for suggesting the lake," Isaiah encroaches on Taylor's thoughts when he joins her.

"It's not Lake Tahoe, but glad you enjoy," she muses.

He removes the shades and stares at her, "Tahoe is not off the table." Her eyes warm as she touches his arm, as if to concede. Her touch electrocutes him, causing him to lose resolve. He wants her. They create a beautiful buzz of sexual tension, and it floats in the air.

"Is it too much, me laying next to you in a swimsuit," Taylor breaks the silence. She changed into a seductive two-piece with a cutout front. It has one spaghetti strap and one suspender strap on each shoulder, with a matching high-waist bottom.

Isaiah tries to focus his eyes on something other than Taylor. All he wants is to peel it off her. "Well," he rummages for words. "Yes, it is." The plea in his eyes demonstrates his struggle with restraint. "I want to kiss every inch of you, peeling that cloth off of you with each kiss," he admits.

Rising to sit face-to-face with him, "What do you want from me?" Taylor isn't naïve to the urging they both feel. No guy made her feel the stimulation in her body the way Isaiah does.

"I told you what I want." Isaiah knows she means beyond this moment, but he cannot think straight. The torment his restraint is causing him is crumbling his sentences, and his resolve is fading fast. He cups her face and speaks slowly and deliberately. "I cannot stop thinking of you, and I cannot shake the memory of what we shared. I don't want to."

His confession warms her heart. She rises, interweaves her hands around his neck, and rests her forehead against his. "I can't stop thinking of you," her whisper lingers on his lips. Isaiah's body elevates with desire as he inhales her breath.

Bringing her hands to his chiseled chest, Taylor releases his neck and traces the fine lines of his muscles as her fingers brush through the raised hairs. He tilts her head to engulf her mouth with his. His pleasure is heard through his groans as he pulls her body over to straddle his lap. They give in to their longing with nothing but the lake and rip tides surrounding them. The passion from their slow, deliberate moves coupled with the radiant sun creates a coat of sweat on their bodies. Satisfaction ripples against the tides as their cries of relief ricochet in the air when they reach their climax.

Each one seeks to regain control of their body as they lay bare beneath the sun. "Can passersby see us?" Taylor's concern is sudden.

"Can anybody see us?" Isaiah howls into the open air, his words vibrating across the lake.

A slow resounding *yes* returns, and the two scramble for cover. Their sail on the lake ends as they watch the prominent sky form into a horizon of blue, purple, and orange streaks as the sun sets.

The ride back to the city is quiet. Both are lost in their thoughts of each other. Their inhibitions are unconfined, and their passion is liberated.

"Mr. Hunt, this is Isaiah. Isaiah, this is my real-life guardian angel." Taylor focuses on Mr. Hunt's observations of Isaiah. Rarely does she bring anyone home, but when she does, he makes it his mission to sniff him out.

"It's nice to make your acquaintance. May I offer you something to drink?" Mr. Hunt x-rays Isaiah for traits he deems unacceptable but, more importantly, to see if Taylor glows.

"Likewise, Mr. Hunt." Isaiah shakes the older gents' hand, believing Mr. Hunt added a warning squeeze toward the end.

Taylor never asked Mr. Hunt how he discerns if the guy isn't right for her. Somehow, he knows. He'd say, "Unacceptable," without further explanation. When Taylor defied and continued to date, he wouldn't say a word until the guy was no longer. She'd ask, "How did you know?" Mr. Hunt's response was always the same. "Age and wisdom."

"Will our guest join us for dinner?" Mr. Hunt asks Taylor. She now knows Mr. Hunt flagged questionable traits. He never stays for dinner. Sharing dinnertime with Mrs. Hunt is precious to him.

"Yes, Isaiah will stay for dinner." It bothers her Mr. Hunt signaled undesirable qualities from Isaiah. She's opening up to him. She likes him. But Mr. Hunt's never been wrong about a guy she dated. She hopes this time he is.

Taylor shows Isaiah to the living quarters, where he settles in. While Isaiah showers, she goes to her office. She can't shake the thought the anonymous caller was at her center. Spreading out the collections of the case file across her desk, she zooms in on the photograph. As she studies it, she calls Joe. "Joe, I sent you a photo. Will you validate its realness? And, I need to know who took it?"

"I'm on it, Ms. T." Joe called her Ms. T since high school. When her dad was involved in ominous cases, Joe was her detail. She appreciated him allowing her to be a teenager, but he was never more than a few feet away—no one knew, including her friends. After her father's death, she named

Joe head of her detail. She trusts Joe, and he knows neither she nor Mr. Hunt like the attention.

After providing Joe specifics, Taylor analyzes the photo. It is Boyd's car, no question, and it's at the top of the mountains. Who took the photo? There is no date or time stamp on it. She is optimistic the conglomerate's team will discover the truth. As she wraps up, Isaiah strides into her office. Discreetly, she slides the print under the papers on her desk. Mr. Daniels does not want the mayor to know of the photo. She's uncertain why; nevertheless, she cannot reveal it to Isaiah. "Hi, you're all cleaned up?"

"Yes, your shower is off the chain. I can do some things in it."

"Ha! I'll quickly shower and change. Dinner should be ready by then." Taylor comes around the desk and leads Isaiah out of her office.

"Want me to join you?" he asks, half teasing.

Taylor giggles at Isaiah's proposition. "You can keep Mr. Hunt company. He will show you the wine room."

"You have a wine room?"

"It's more like a pantry. You'll see." The blossoming lovers inhale the aromas of dinner as they approach the kitchen. "Mr. H, do you mind showing Isaiah the wine room? I'll be ready for dinner shortly." Mr. Hunt signals to Taylor, and she is off to the shower.

Isaiah selects a Malbec from the wine pantry. While the wine breathes, he lurks to Taylor's office. He was sure she hid something when he came in a few minutes ago. What could it be? And why didn't she want him to know what it was? Shuffling the papers, he exposes the photo. "Goddamn it!" As he held the picture, memories of the fateful night rushed to the forefront of his mind.

He eased Boyd's Bugatti out of the garage of their child-hood home. Boyd was in Maui. So this is Isaiah's opportunity to drive his car. Boyd repeatedly told him he couldn't handle the blistering speed. But he would never know. Isaiah entered the highway, thinking he might pick up a girl. Sitting behind the wheel of the most lavish supercar ever made boosted his confidence.

He was soaring through the red light when he noticed reflections of blue lights. Checking the rearview mirror, he confirmed it was an LAPD unmarked car. Not realizing the cruiser was after him, he eased into the slow lane, freeing the passing lane. The cruiser followed. "Holy shit!" he remembers exclaiming. He was being stopped. He pulled over and watched in the side mirror as the officer approached the car.

"Good evening, Officer." He remembers observing the officer's badge. His name is Franklin.

"License, registration, and proof of insurance," the officer stipulated.

"Yes sir, Officer Franklin. May I ask why you stopped me? The light wasn't red."

In a more deliberate tone and much slower, "License, registration, and proof of insurance," Officer Franklin commanded.

"My license is in my wallet, in my jacket. It's on the passenger seat. The registration is in the glove box. I will reach for my license first. Is that okay?" Isaiah knows the rules. Keep your hands in sight and announce every move.

"Yes, get your license first," Officer Franklin demands. He remembered fidgeting to get his license out of the slot of his wallet. There's no time to wonder why he stopped him anymore; it's survival mode. Just follow his orders, and all will be well. He hands the officer his license and then retrieves the registration and insurance from the glove box.

"Step out of the car, sir," Officer Franklin orders.

"Why?" Isaiah hopes this isn't a setup. There were rumors that officers profiled drivers of luxurious cars for bogus charges. Now he's driving one of the most high-end sports cars ever made. It's not even his.

"Get out of the car!" Isaiah doesn't protest. He belligerently opens the car door, forcing Officer Franklin to hop back.

"Step to the back of your vehicle."

"Aw, come on!"

"Back of the vehicle, now!" Isaiah steps to the back of the car where the lights of the unmarked LAPD cruiser shine on him. He hopes the dashboard camera is powered on.

"Man, this is B.S. I can take a Breathalyzer. I haven't been drinking. I touch my nose. Do you want me to walk backward? What is it you want me to do?"

"I stopped you because you were speeding, and your plate is expired."

Isaiah recalls looking down at the expired license plate. Why the hell would Boyd not renew his plate? "I can explain."

"Shut up and open your trunk?"

"For what?" Isaiah recollects he didn't know how to open the trunk. This isn't his car. Officer Franklin throws him against the back of the sports car with no warning, forcefully pressing his face into the trunk.

"What the hell is wrong with you?" The officer applied more weight and pressed his face harder into the trunk's cold metal. "I know my rights. My uncle is the mayor..."

Officer Franklin pulls his gun and pushes it into the back of Isaiah's neck. The cold barrel forms a crease in his skin. He inhales, afraid if he breathes, he dies. "Don't speak!" Isaiah listens. Officer Franklins lifts Isaiah's head off the trunk without removing the gun. "Is this car stolen?" Isaiah is terrified to answer; he told him not to speak. "Get on your knees and place your hands behind your back." Isaiah does as he says, and the gun is no longer in his neck. He doesn't know what came over him. When Officer Franklin reached for his cuffs, Isaiah bum-rushed him. They fought, and during their struggle Officer Franklin's gun fired.

Isaiah scrambled to Boyd's car as Officer Franklin's body lies in a pool of blood. He is scared shitless. No one will believe this is an accident. "Uncle, I am in trouble." He doesn't remember dialing the mayor.

"What's wrong..."

"He's dead! I think he's dead. I didn't mean to shoot him."

The mayor can't make sense of his nephew's rambling. "Isaiah, where are you? Who's dead?"

"The officer. He stopped me and..."

"Isaiah, listen to me and listen to me carefully. Do exactly as I say." The mayor instructs Isaiah and tells him the Fixer will come to help him.

Taylor finds Isaiah in her office holding the photograph of Boyd's car in the mountains. "Isaiah, why are you meddling through my work?" She immediately remembers Hansen asking if Isaiah could be the shooter.

She startles him. He jumps out of his daydream. "What..."

"Why are you snooping in my office? And why do you look like you've seen a ghost?"

Isaiah is nervous. Her tone is accusatory. "Counselor..."

"Answer me!" Isaiah is stumped.

"Do you have insights into the photograph you're holding?" He doesn't realize he's still holding the picture and hastily drops it on the desk.

Mr. Hunt yells to Taylor she has a call from her father's firm. "This conversation isn't over." She escorts him out of her office as she responds to Mr. Hunt. Taylor takes the call from her living room as Mr. Hunt lays the place settings on the dining room table. Isaiah sits at the wet bar where he opened the wine before going into Taylor's office. He needs bourbon now.

Walking into the kitchen where Isaiah sits, Taylor is fueled by emotions. Joe gave her a lead to explore while his team gathers the information she needs. When she reaches the kitchen, she stands eye-to-eye with Isaiah. "Did you or did you not have something to do with Detective Franklin's shooting?" Mr. Hunt stops in his tracks when he overhears Taylor.

Isaiah stands from the barstool. He is unrecognizable. His look is suspicious, and his demeanor exudes rage. When Taylor questions him, he takes a threatening step toward her to intimidate her. She is firm in her stance, although trembling inside. She cannot predict his next move. Isaiah does not answer but again steps toward her, closing the space between them. He lifts her chin and, with a firm whisper, "It behooves you to let sleeping dogs lie."

Concealing the fear stirring inside of her, she hisses, "Are you the sleeping dog I lie with?" Taylor does not blink or show any emotion; neither does he. After an undetermined amount of time elapses, he snatches his keys from the counter where they stand and storms out of the kitchen.

A few seconds later, the elevator closes behind him as he hurls obscene language.

Her knees are weakened. She slumbers against the kitchen counter, sliding to the floor. The unction in her gut tells her the man she's falling in love with knows something about Detective Franklin's shooting. With no evidence yet to prove Isaiah's involvement, she weeps. Mr. Hunt sits next to Taylor and cradles her in his arms. "You will know the truth soon enough. I will stay with you tonight."

Heaving wind and rain wake Taylor on Saturday morning. She promised Dulaney to hang out today, but she wants nothing more than to stay in bed. Sounds of pots and the smell of bacon suggest Mr. Hunt is cooking breakfast. Scampering to the kitchen, "No, no, no. It's your day off. Go home. I am fine." Mr. Hunt utters not a word until her pancakes, bacon, and mimosa are on the breakfast counter.

"Now, your favorites," and he smiles like a proud grandpa. "I will see you on Monday, right?" Mr. Hunt isn't sure of Taylor's travel plans after her ordeal with Isaiah.

"Yes, I will be here on Monday but spend the day with Mrs. Hunt. I'll grab breakfast on the go."

"Very well. Get some rest; you didn't sleep well." Mr. Hunt put his hat on and called the driver from the pad on the wall. He informed the concierge to let no one in Taylor's unit without his clearance on his way out.

Taylor climbed back in bed. Mr. Hunt was right; she didn't sleep at all last night. Isaiah's words rang in her ear continuously. *It behooves you to let sleeping dogs lie.* WTH.

Taylor hibernates the weekend, avoiding all calls. Unbeknownst to her, Mr. Hunt instructed the concierge to clear all guests through him. He suspected Isaiah might return.

On Monday morning, Taylor starts her day by stopping at Alexander Legal Services, hoping the team completed its due diligence on the photo. She suspects whatever's in the package Joe compiles, she'll need time to process. It is unnerving to think Isaiah had something to do with the crime. If he did, Joe is sure to discover it. Taking a seat in the chair behind her father's old desk, she senses she is one step closer to revealing the truth. "Ah, Daddy! I miss you so much!"

"He would be proud of you," Joe encourages her as he steps inside the doorway.

"Good morning, Joe. I didn't hear you."

"We saw you come in from the cameras. Figured I'd let you know we need a few hours to complete our investigation. Stick around. You are a natural in his chair."

"I can feel his presence in here."

"Good thing you didn't give up his office when you gave up your position. I'll see you later." And Joe is out of sight before she responds.

Taylor reminisces on the times she spent in her father's office as a child. She pretended to be him when he wasn't looking, taking on his stance with her shoulders broaden, exuding confidence before speaking. He was her champion. Her vibrating phone in her pocket brings her back to the present. It's Isaiah for the thousandth time. The nerve of him! She has no doubt he told the mayor about the picture of Boyd's car in the mountains that he saw on her desk.

While she waits for his results, she follows the lead Joe gave her on Friday. It's a dead end. Exasperated, Taylor needs refueling, and she knows just where to get it. A quick call to Chantell, and thirty minutes later, she surprises her kids with donuts and chocolate milk. They jump and pull and push her in every direction. She is sure the donuts will fall to the floor. The kids bring her such joy. They form a circle on the floor with her seated in the middle and share their stories. Coltrane and Chantell appreciate it from afar. Hours later, Kevin ends their reunion, "We don't want new computers, Ms. T. We just want you here with us." Tears cover her face, but she is recharged.

The kids scatter to different areas of the center. Taylor retreats to her office and calls Mr. Daniels. While she updates him, Coltrane lays a manila folder before her. Peeling back the seal and removing the contents, "Oh, my goodness! You won't believe..."

"What is it, Taylor?"

"Mr. Daniels, I will call you back. I need to see the mayor." How could he? She trusted him. He promised her dad he'd look out for her. How could he involve her?

"Taylor, wait..." she abruptly hangs up. Grabbing her keys—thank God she drove her car—she dashes out like a bolt of lightning.

The mayor is on the phone when she storms into his office. She throws the summary her security team prepared, together with photos of Isaiah standing over Detective Franklin's body where he shot him, at the mayor. Papers flew in the air, falling to the desk and floor. "You knew this whole time! How could you?" The mayor doesn't respond but gives her a blank stare.

"Answer me!" Taylor screams at the mayor with tears flowing down her cheeks. Motioning for his secretary to close the door, the mayor stands and walks toward Taylor.

"Don't come near me!"

"Sweetheart, you don't understand."

"You're right about that! I don't understand why my mentor, my dad's friend, used me to cover up a crime. You lied this whole time—talking about Judge Crane seeking revenge on you—I never bought that theory. Yet, it's Isaiah seeking revenge on Boyd. Low and behold, you—the mayor—cover the tracks of one nephew by framing the other. Did you think I wouldn't uncover you and Isaiah's clandestineness?"

"It wasn't like that, Taylor."

The mayor recalls receiving Isaiah's frantic call. It was poker night, and he and his friends were doing their usual—cigars, bourbon, and exotic dancers. He could hardly make sense of his nephew, who was incoherent.

Gaining everyone's attention as he quieted the noise in the room, he tried to make sense of Isaiah's rambling. "What's wrong, Isaiah?"

"I think he's dead. I didn't mean to shoot him. We were tussling over the gun, and..."

"Isaiah, who's dead?"

"The officer. He stopped me and..."

"Listen to me, Isaiah; and listen carefully." Emotions gripped the mayor. Does he protect his nephew from the judicial system wherein he took an oath to uphold the law? He isn't naïve to Isaiah being a young, black man who just shot a police officer? Should the mayor take a blind eye to justice and protect his family? His next decision would take him back to the life he once knew growing up on the streets. He worked hard to overcome the poverty of his past. But his nephew's life is on the line. His faith in the judicial system is now tested.

"Nephew, hold on. I will get help for you." Mayor Sellect recounts what he understood of Isaiah's prolix to his buddies at the poker table. He makes a call he wishes he never had to make.

"Malone, I need your help."

"Anything, man. But these are different times. You cannot get your hands dirty."

"My nephew is in a situation that needs fixing urgently. I will send his coordinates to you. Let me know when it's handled." The mayor goes back to his call with Isaiah.

"Nephew, drop a pin of your location to my phone. And then, put the body in the trunk and get out of sight.

"I don't know how to open the trunk."

"What?" The mayor is befuddled by Isaiah's confession.

"I am in Boyd's car. I don't know how to..."

"Isaiah, you must compose yourself and fast. The Fixer will arrive shortly."

The mayor recalls Isaiah telling him someone showed up to help him. "He's in all black, and his face is covered. How do I know I can trust him?"

"You can trust me. Do as he says, and you will be fine." He remained on the phone while Isaiah followed the Fixer to the Santa Monica Mountains. The following day, Boyd's car was sterilized and returned to its garage.

Taylor's yelling snapped the mayor out of his recollection.

"What was it like, huh? Did you kill the investigator too?" The mayor's look gives Taylor cause for concern. "Holy shit! You know what, I don't want to know. I have no words for you. And I never want to see you or Isaiah again."

"It was the only way, Taylor. No one would ever believe the shooting was an accident. Justice has to be blind in this case. There's no other way to protect Isaiah and Boyd."

"Do you hear yourself? I took an oath to upload the law—and so did you, not take a blind eye to it. You explain to Boyd why I will not defend his post-trial motions." Taylor turns to depart the mayor's office.

"Ms. Alexander, I suggest you rethink your decision."

"Or what? Don't dare threaten me! How would my dad feel knowing his long-time friend manipulated his daughter to save himself? Go to hell!"

Taylor's emotions are scattered as she rushes out of the mayor's office to her car. How could he do this to her? She sits in her car in total dismay. Where is his moral compass? Fumes emit from her at the thought of the mayor and Isaiah's conniving behavior. They volleyed, and she was their tennis ball. Never has she been betrayed to this degree.

She guns the accelerator and swerves onto the highway. Isaiah calls. She presumes the mayor warned him and yelled into the speaker, "Where are you?" Her adrenaline is pumping and her pulse racing.

"Taylor, it was..."

She cuts him off, shrieking into the speakers. "Where are you?"

Unable to stomach her hurt, "I am at the Waldorf Astoria." She says nothing, and he hears the dial tone within seconds. Her cold, formidable voice caused the hairs on Isaiah's arms to rise. He threw his phone across the room, crashing it against the wall. He needed something or someone to blame. Hell, he blamed himself for her pain.

Staring at the hotel's entrance from her car, she contemplates. Should she confront Isaiah? Does it matter? It nauseates her to think what they shared was a lie. Taylor's nerves are shot. Her stomach revolts. Rage eats at her, the heated fury boiling in her veins.

She must be a colossal fool, is what she sensationalizes. Only a fool would talk to Isaiah after this revelation. Maybe it doesn't matter because what she wants to do is slap the shit out of him; not talk. Taylor fought the water welling in her eyes, but a single tear slid down her round cheek. Numbness is overtaking her emotions. If only her dad was here to guide her through this mess. He'd know what to do—about the mayor and Isaiah. Sniveling, *"Daddy, I wish you were here,"* she drives off and heads home. Isaiah doesn't deserve her tears or time. He can descend to the underworld, right along with his uncle.

When the elevator opens to her unit, Mr. Hunt stands before her with his coat and hat in hand. Surprised to see him because he wasn't supposed to work today, she sobs and collapses in his arms. She is safe now. Her barriers are down, and the adrenaline rush dissipated.

"I got you, baby girl." Mr. Hunt knows her tears have to do with Isaiah. He's comforted her many times when relationships ended, but this cry is different. She is broken.

"Your hurt will pass with time."

He is wrong. She can't imagine not hurting. The mayor was her mentor, her father's friend. Yet, he and Isaiah engineered a plan to save themselves, manipulating her in the process. This hurt is deep beneath her skin.

Taylor raises her head to Mr. Hunt's compassion and explains how the mayor used her to clear Boyd of an attempted murder charge; all the while knowing Isaiah was the shooter. Mr. Hunt has wrath in his eyes. He pours a glass of wine for Taylor and encourages her to relax, assuring her he will return after he finishes the errands.

"I don't know what I would do without you." Taylor thanks Mr. Hunt and fails at convincing him he need not return. The radiant sun beamed through the window as she stared out into the city. Taylor thought, there's nothing perfect about love and life, but must Isaiah play her for a fool. He portrayed himself as the epitome of the man of her dreams, and she fell for it. If there is a silver lining, she finally—after years of guarding her emotions—allowed herself to love. She'd like to say and be loved, but she was a plot for Isaiah.

When Mr. Hunt enters the lobby on his way out, Isaiah argues with the concierge who informed him, "I'm sorry, sir. We have instructions not to allow you to Ms. Alexander's unit."

Isaiah has no shame. He wants her back. All the times they shared flashed through his mind, followed by an ache of loss radiating through his body. He spots Mr. Hunt as he exits the elevator. "Sir, is Taylor home?"

"Good day, Mr. Isaiah. You are not to come around here."

"But, sir. Will you please call her?" Isaiah understands Mr. Hunt's vacillation to trust him, given the circumstances. But if he could just explain.

"No, Mr. Isaiah, I will not call her, and you are never to call her again." Isaiah knows he brought this on himself, and he knows it looks terrible. But he fell in love with her—deception or not. He wanted to tell her. Several times, he tried to tell her.

"Mr. Hunt, I need to speak with her."

"Mr. Isaiah, every action is met with a corresponding reaction. You young people don't consider the consequences of your ways, until it's too late. Reflect on this as a growth opportunity—make better choices as you forge ahead in life. This is the best advice I can offer you. Now leave her alone. You broke her. Good day."

The feeling in Isaiah's stomach is reminiscent of a gut-punch. The kind old man's words pierced his soul. He'd lost her. Shaking his head with understanding, he left Taylor's building with a heavy heart.